# To Love a
# REDNECK

*with love*
*Dea Renaye*

## DEA RENAYE

ISBN 978-1-63874-020-9 (paperback)
ISBN 978-1-63874-021-6 (digital)

Copyright © 2021 by Dea Renaye

All rights reserved. No part of this publication may be reproduced, distributed, or transmitted in any form or by any means, including photocopying, recording, or other electronic or mechanical methods without the prior written permission of the publisher. For permission requests, solicit the publisher via the address below.

Christian Faith Publishing, Inc.
832 Park Avenue
Meadville, PA 16335
www.christianfaithpublishing.com

Printed in the United States of America

Not all of this book is total imagination and fiction. Norm and Edie were actual mushroom pickers I met in my research.

My family, my husband and my children, grandchildren and great-grandchildren, and friends are all loving and responsible and surely some of the greatest people in the world! To them I dedicate this book. To have family one can be proud of is a priceless, rich treasure and God's greatest gift to me.

# Chapter 1

"The baby is coming right now!" Hysteria threatened Amber's mother, Gert. "We can't make it to the hospital. The doctor won't come here. He wants to meet us at the hospital!" She'd had three previous hospital births. One where the nurse had cruelly held her legs together in an attempt to stop the baby until the doctor was ready for her. Another baby was nearly burnt by a too hot water bottle meant to keep it warm. None of the births was easy due mainly to the barbaric practices of a few nurses and doctors who she was unfortunate enough to have attending her. Her fear from past experiences was understandable.

Amber's father, Rob, calmed her mother enough to get her into their bed. He informed the family doctor that the baby was indeed going to be born at home. The country doctor had been to their home several times before when their oldest daughter, Andrea, was seriously ill, and it was closer than the hospital for him anyhow. Rob assured his wife that he would help her deliver if the doctor didn't make it in time. Amber came into the world in the bed in which she was conceived, with less stress than the doctor-assisted births had given Gert. Her father's only training had been in helping their many farm animals give birth. The family doctor did come soon after, roughly ensuring the afterbirth was discharged completely and there were no complications. He refused to process and sign a birth certificate in his seeming anger at Amber's inappropriate arrival. Also, he had not been there when she had first been born.

So now with four children, a struggling dairy farm to run, and only a kindly sister-in-law to help for a week, Amber's hardworking parents carried on as best they could. Though her birth was never registered, Amber did receive a baptism certificate from their church soon after she was born.

Can a child know from birth that they are not going to be easily acknowledged? To feel apologetic for causing distress, anger, and extra work? Be fearful of acceptance? Amber tried to be good, obey her parents, and to learn what she admired in her older sisters and brother. Still, she always felt that somehow she didn't belong like they did. She was always the baby who didn't know as much as they did. They were capable at so many more things than she was. She often kept in the background, staying timid and shy.

Amber so looked forward to the first day of school, thinking she would come home able to read and write like her older sisters and brother. A week later, she was still at their mercy. She couldn't even read the funny papers. She was always too little and too dumb. Even her slightly younger neighbor girlfriend preferred her older sister's company to hers. It was always better to stay out of the way, or be willing to take orders, if there was more than one person around her.

Laughter soon embarrassed Amber. The older children knew so much more than her and laughed at, and ridiculed, her often made mistakes. On April Fools' Day, she participated in a joke. She was to go to the barn where her parents were working, to tell a tale, and then to count to ten before saying "April Fool." She did a superb job of telling the story. As her mother started to react, she continued to count out loud to ten to say "April Fool!" Her siblings knew she would ruin the joke! When she wanted to spell her friend Robin's name, she asked instead how to spell *raw* and *bun*. It didn't look quite how she'd seen Robin spell it. How she wished to be smarter.

"What does *F* mean, Amber?" she was asked on a family outing.

"Fun?" She guessed it started with the *f* sound.

"No, something bad, *f, f,*" said her smarter sibling.

"Fart!" That was the very worst word she'd heard ever.

"*F, f, f.* Guess again," was the patience losing request.

Exasperated and desperately wanting to fit in, Amber blurted, "Farting, f——ing, fun!" to a roar of laughter in which even her parents quietly joined.

She anxiously asked, "Was I right? Am I right?" Finally, her sympathetic sister, Andrea, agreed that she was right, but the snickering continued.

Amber gathered the chicken eggs and sat on the couch with them carefully under her. "*Prrrck, perrrucck, perrruucckk.*" She tried to sound like a chicken on a nest. "Get the eggs, Mom. Get the eggs." She flapped her arms. Gert humored her by pretending to gather eggs. Amber had to repeat her request before Gert actually reached far enough under her to feel the still warm eggs and broke out in shocked laughter. Everyone thought it was a great funny joke, but Amber became embarrassed almost to tears.

Small for her age and easily bullied, Amber still had good friends in school despite her awkward shyness. Other children often enjoyed a companion who was content not to be the center of attention and was eager to accommodate and please them. Of course, if someone became one too many, "Well, sorry, Amber, see you later." Boys especially though, being naturally more dominant or protective, paid particular attention to her. Some were bullies who her two-years-older, self-assured sister, April, protected her from. She learned to accept good-natured teasing from others or their enthusiastic renditions of accomplishments. After all, her siblings always protected her from others and looked out for her even if they had a few laughs at her expense.

# Chapter 2

Andrew was a month younger than Amber and was also small for his age. He came to visit, from Northern Canada, and stayed with his sister, brother-in-law, and their young family (who Amber and April occasionally babysat for) on their dairy farm just south of the US border, near Mason, every summer. He started hanging around with Amber and helping her with her chores. They developed a comfortable friendship, picking the thorn-filled wild blackberries, hiking up the mountainside along the railroad tracks, and doing other things together.

"Do you dare me?" Andrew asked. "Do you double dare me?" They had finished Amber's chores and were sitting together on the hay bales stored in the upstairs of the barn. He'd wanted to be alone with her in a secret place but wouldn't say why.

"What?" Amber replied. "Dare you what?" She enjoyed Andrew's attraction to her, but he was a whole month younger, so she didn't take it seriously. Andrew only repeated his insistent serious question.

"Sure, okay, I dare you," Amber was curious.

Andrew moved toward her, and she still had no idea of what he was about to do. "Do you double dare me?" He smiled.

"Okay." She was getting impatient to discover the mystery. "I double dare you!" They were about ten years old, both shy, but never awkward together.

Andrew reached for her and kissed her. She liked her surprising first kiss, but now they were suddenly awkward together. Andrew remembered his sister was expecting him back soon. Even as he quickly left, he seemed to have a special grin that said, "Wow! I did it!"

When summer was over, they soon started writing each other, ending their letters with *xoxoxo*. Andrew was good for Amber's ego. They remained friends in the summers when he came back, but future kisses were avoided by Amber. After all, he was younger—and a Canadian.

Amber and her sister April walked or caught a ride a mile from their farm into Mason whenever they could. The small US border town boasted of many churches, a movie theater, bowling alley, roller skating rink, baseball park, cafes, and bars for entertainment. It was the rink for them! They saved their berry-picking and babysitting money to rent skates and race around the large wooden floor in circles. Amber loved weaving in and around the slower, and few faster, skaters as fast as she could go. The skater who stood out the most on her way around was a tall gangly boy. His arms and legs were going every which way as he helplessly tried to keep his balance on the unmanageable wheeled skates. He often retreated back to the rails on the walls as he made his way around the rink.

Amber went back to the area set up for changing from shoes to skates to retie her skate that had come untied. When she looked up, the gangly young boy was there. He complimented her on her skating.

"I ice-skate real good, but this is so different that I'm having trouble getting used to it," he said. "There's lots of ice to play hockey on where we usually live. My aunt"—he pointed to an older teenage girl—"and I walked across the border 'cause she wanted to come skating here. Sometimes we go to a movie show. It takes an hour to walk here. We have to check in at the border, but they always let us come across when we tell them what we're going to do. Do you live here? We have lots of relatives who live near here, and Dad brought our family here to find work during spring breakup for a while. You can't log when everything is thawing. Two of our houses burnt down from chimney fires already, and even with wood heat, the house we're in now is pretty cold in the winter. Not as cold as our outhouse though. Mom is having another baby too, so it's good to be near a bigger hospital. Is living in the US any different than living in Canada?"

He was so friendly and easy to talk to that Amber shyly told him that her sister and she had also walked an hour from their farm but had never gone to a movie. She thought his aunt was pretty but didn't look old enough to be an aunt. She was eighteen, and he was six years younger. Amber did the math—that meant he was her sister April's age. She offered to skate with him to help him get his balance. They skated the final door prize skate together where another couple won the prize by being under the right light when the music stopped. He was so enthusiastic and funny. Future plans to go to a movie together were discussed. Soon the night was over, and it was time to walk back home. They never again saw each other at the rink, though.

Over the years, other boys had approached and dated Amber. When they found out she wouldn't neck on the first date and could hardly carry on a conversation either, they lost interest. Gradually she came to believe she was quite inferior to most others and not at all pretty. She had long ago buried the memories, but somehow, guilt and shame followed her through her life from her participation in exploring the temptation of "you show me yours, I'll show you mine" sexual curiosity of innocent young children (started by trusted older persons). She was unaware of the subconscious protective distance she grew to maintain or where its root cause started.

Andrea, April, and Amber picked berries for income every summer since they were small. With that and their babysitting money, they could shop for new school clothes in the fall. Ryan, their brother, hired out to other farms with the hay crimper that Rob had bought to give their hay crop a flatter, fluffier, better chance of drying between the frequent rains. There was always more love than money available to the hardworking farm family.

Farmwork included milking cows, harvesting hay to feed them, growing most of their own food, and raising pigs and chickens for meat. Old milk cows that no longer produced enough milk were also butchered for meat. Homemade bread, fresh from the oven, was a favorite snack. (Once, the children took the entire crust from around the whole loaf instead of arguing for the crust. Gert only laughed and toasted the loaf's remains.) For a special treat, one of a "six for twenty-six cents" candy bar was cut up and shared. They ate well, if not fancy, and were healthy and strong.

Farm families developed many do-it-yourself skills. In those days, girls had to wear modest dresses to school. If they had their eye on a too expensive one in the Sears catalogue, their mother would sew them one in a similar fashion. The girls helped Mom reupholster furniture and do other interior designing in their home. Machine and vehicle maintenance was second nature to Rob, and he taught his quick-learning son, Ryan. Rob, with Ryan's help, designed and built his own fishing and speed boat along with water skis, surfboard, and even oars. Such family fun! Gert loved music, so a milk cow was traded for a player piano. They all had to take piano lessons, but it was easier and more fun to put a piano roll in and pump the peddles. They would pass their hands over the keys pretending to be great musicians.

Work hard, be responsible, love and play well, and use common sense were ingrained in their upbringing. If they asked to participate in a questionable activity, their parents made them think for themselves by asking them what they would want their own children to do. Go to church when possible and live out your belief in God. Rob had no use for the self-righteous preachers or educated idiots who condemned making use of God's provisions. He'd rather be in his field haying and thanking God for the good weather than piously in church thinking about the rain coming to destroy his crop. He'd walk up to total strangers on fishing trips to make a friendly comment about the beautiful world God created. Gert added the responsibility of being a 4-H leader (head, heart, hands, and health incentives) to her busy life and was a loving, available, influence on many lives. Many girls felt more confidence in sharing their growing-up concerns with Gert than with their own parents.

Rob and Gert showed the belief they held in everyday living. Prayers and Bible reading attended their main meal of the day. Their example allowed Amber to answer a young visiting missionary that it might not be what God wanted for her when he insisted that she follow his example and become a missionary like him when she matured. She thought God might want her more for the few lost sheep than the multitudes. God had had to take his intended bride away to heaven in order to get him to be obedient, he'd warned her.

Amber was to play Mary in the Christmas play. One of the deacons leered at her small frame and crudely remarked, "How are you going to be able to breastfeed the baby Jesus?" Being a small late developer, she was often referred to as the nameless "little Condor sister" and took imagined insults personally. Her older sisters were voluptuous, witty, and self-assured. It seemed she was not as important and noticeable as they were for themselves.

Andrea, April, and Ryan made good use of the skills they learned. They were popular in school and achieved good grades. Andrea graduated and went to college. She roomed with two other college girls and worked at a burger joint to earn her own way. April soon followed in her footprints.

After Ryan graduated from high school, he had moved in with buddies who worked in the pipe fitting apprenticeship with him. When he bought himself a motorcycle and gave Amber a ride, she was totally thrilled. Bert, his friend, had come to visit the farm with Ryan for the weekend. He teased Amber that he was going to take her out on a date when she grew up. When he saw how much she enjoyed getting a ride on Ryan's motorcycle, he secretly gave Ryan a deal on his old motor scooter. Amber was to receive it for Christmas.

Amber was elated and rode it as fast as it would go (about fifty miles an hour). She couldn't drive it on any of the main roads in Mason, but she could drive it to friends' houses and to the raspberry patch to pick every summer. She never wore a helmet or any protective clothing to ride. The closest she came to getting hurt was when the back wheel flew off when she hit a railroad bump too hard and fast. She kept the bike upright until she got it stopped and retrieved the wheel. She walked home for help. After it was fixed, she slowed down for bumps.

With Amber being the only one left home, the farmwork was getting to be a heavy load for Gert. Rob hired help now and then, but they mostly managed by themselves. Amber was planning to find work when she graduated from high school but still live at home to help with the farm. She had been a good berry picker, receiving the bonus for picking over a ton of raspberries several seasons, and even got another job in the afternoon shift at the cannery (She'd received the required social insurance card and number by producing school records and her baptism certificate). She was happy to be able to save money and pay her own expenses.

# Chapter 3

As a farmer's only son, Ryan would have been eligible to reject the summons to enter the military with the Vietnam War push. The easy way out, however, was not the way his conscience led. Rob and Ryan decided to take a fishing trip through the wilds of Canada. They would visit Andrew's parents on their trip. A break from working to build their special memories before Ryan enlisted and was sent to boot camp training.

Gert and Amber looked after the farm with the help of a hired hand while they were gone. Rob and Ryan came back home excited! Not about the fish they caught, though. They had found a rustic tourist resort on a large, deep pristine lake in a quaint northern town called Tesley. If they sold the farm, the Condors could easily buy it. Apparently it was meant to be—the farm sold.

After twenty-five years of farming, Rob and Gert made the decision to immigrate to Canada. Amber, still underage and finishing high school, was also immigrating. Rob and Gert Condor bought the resort in the remote town in British Columbia. A neighbor had a haul truck they could rent as a moving van. The last of the farm equipment and livestock were sold. Pets were given away. After years of accumulation, hand-drawn pictures, school papers, and other keepsake treasures had to be packed or given away, or discarded and burnt. It seemed Gert had treasured and kept every memento of her children's efforts as they grew. Finally, the ones she couldn't part with were boxed and loaded. Their furniture went carefully into the haul truck. Years of home canning was packed up to go as well as two freezers full of food. Amber's motor scooter was also fit in.

Amber's favorite very old car went to her aunt and uncle. She was to stay at her widowed grandfather's home and drive another family car to and from school in the following months until she graduated from high school.

First though, the day long big "wagon train" move during spring break. Andrea, Ryan, April, and Amber would help with the over four-hundred-mile move by driving a vehicle loaded to the max, while Rob and Gert took the haul truck. Clearing US and Canadian customs was long and difficult, but they all made it through. Rob and Gert were to take the lead, while Ryan would watch out for his sisters by following behind. Along the way, the driver of a sports car attempted to force Amber's car to a stop but sped off when her brother drove up. Then Andrea's car got stuck between the gears. Ryan crawled under it to haywire a fix, while the sisters watched. What a good plan it was for the siblings to stay in sight of each other. The long road north would have been too lonely and scary otherwise. The last sixty miles, traveling slowly, were on a rough, narrow, winding, bumpy, dusty, gravel road that seemed to go on forever. At last they were there, everyone had made it. Two rustic cabins had been prepared for them to sleep in. Grateful and exhausted, they didn't bother to start unloading.

The ex-owners came to greet them again the next morning. She was a petite pretty woman and he a giant of a man with hands as big as a baseball glove. Both were friendly and helpful with unloading some of the major items. The player piano especially needed the extra help. Then, after explaining some of their home and business, the ex-owners packed up their few remaining belongings and wished the new owners well.

Gert was overwhelmed—what were they going to do with all the furniture and everything they'd brought with? Rob needed to return the haul truck as soon as possible, so they'd have to figure something out.

The house that was to be the Condor's new home had a large (roof covered) deck which included a generous wood box. Inside was a sizable kitchen and living room area with a door opening to the large bedroom behind it. There was cold running water for the kitchen sink in the middle of large cupboards. A wood stove with a water reservoir was the heat and hot water source. There was an outhouse out of the bedroom back door, next to a large woodshed. Upstairs, two rooms were only accessible by going outside to the narrow stairs at the backside of the house.

From a rambling four-bedroom farmhouse with indoor plumbing to such rustic, cramped quarters was a great challenge, especially for Gert. Somehow, dressers were stacked upon each other in the kitchen area. Piano and fridge were side by side against one kitchen wall. The electric stove (Rob would wire it in as soon as possible) went beside the wood stove. The well-made large expandable wooden table and chairs took up the remaining space. Two beds and more dressers were added to the wood cabinet commode that had been left in the bedroom. Some of the excess furniture went to the upstairs of the house. (Amber would be able to have a room there to herself.) Whatever more excess would be stored in the upstairs of a boathouse (where some remained for many busy years). Extension cords were run to the woodshed to plug in the freezers. At least all of the resort had electricity.

The six well-built furnished cabins had one or two bedrooms with a closet and a small dresser, with a curtain for its door. The combination living room-kitchen had a wood and small propane stove. There was a sink in the cupboards, but the water had to be gotten from a shared conveniently placed outside tap. Couch, table, chairs, and regular kitchen needs were supplied. Each roof-covered deck had a wood box that was kept filled for the patron's use. Outhouses were a short distance between cabins. The central shower house had two private showers available where a unique wood stove, with copper water pipes inside, heated the gravity fed water and kept the place warm. There were three docks to tie up water craft and swim between. Except for winter, they had a steady clientele who booked their vacations to enjoy the rustic, comfortable, lakeside, wilderness cabins. The lack of modern conveniences was part of the charm. The cabin rent was very reasonable. A campground was also available for tents and house trailers.

The party line telephone in their new home would ring three short and one long if it was for them and could be answered at anywhere in Tesley that had a phone. It was truly like going back fifty years in time for the newcomers. More modern improvements were planned and started right away.

Gert and Amber worked together in the large wash house after saying goodbye to Andrea, April, and Ryan. It boasted a temperamental gas-powered wringer washing machine that would be used along with their electric wringer washing machine to do the laundry for the entire resort, as well as their own. There was electricity and cold running water to the sinks, but a wood stove was there to provide hot water from the large containers on top. Wash day, they would heat water to fill the gas machine for washing the loads and fill the electric one with mainly cold water to rinse. Two clotheslines on pulleys reached from the wash house across the yard to sturdy trees. No such thing as a clothes dryer. Even so, Gert felt more up to her new workload than the farmwork she'd left behind. Doors were always kept closed to discourage curious bears that were occasionally seen passing through their laundry area. Amber was less afraid to shoo them away than her mother was. People were more scary than animals to her.

Rob drove the haul truck back with Amber following in the car she would use to get to school from her grandfather's house. The other children had driven the car that Rob would exchange for the haul truck and drive back to Tesley to rejoin Gert.

# Chapter 4

When Amber came back to the resort after finishing high school, she helped with the workload. She came out of the wash house with her basket of freshly folded laundry. A tall young stranger was getting out of his battered antique car.

"You've got something all over the back of your pants," he said in a friendly voice.

Instinctively, Amber set her basket on the picnic table in front of his car. She brushed her hands across the back of her jeans. She tried to see what he was looking at so intently.

"Still there!" He grinned. "It's my eyes." He slapped his leg, laughing at his own joke.

"Now I'm embarrassed," was Amber's naive reply. She blushed prettily, innocently unaware that her statement could be referring to where his eyes had undressed her.

"What do you think of the price of rice in China?" He grinned at her.

"What?" Amber blinked. "I've never really thought about it," she answered honestly. "What do you think about it?"

He laughed, one of those hearty, funny laughs that were almost impossible not to laugh with. "Do you think the rain will hurt the rhubarb?"

*No*, thought Amber, *the rhubarb are growing well, dependent on a bit of rain. What weird questions…and why is he still laughing till tears almost come out of his twinkly hazel eyes?* Her mouth opened speechless.

"It's just something us guys say to start a conversation," he choked out, seeing her puzzled open-mouth stare. "I'm Cody Bentley. I live here. Just curious to meet the new owners here. So thought I'd drive my car through for a tour. I have a regular car but need to take this one out for a run now and then so it doesn't seize up."

"I absolutely love your car!" Amber exclaimed. "It's older than my '48 old car that we couldn't bring with us." She'd fallen in love with the car at first sight. It was a '37 Chevy with suicide doors.

Soon Cody was telling her more about the town, his family, and the group of young people who got together when they weren't working or going to school. He encouraged her to join them. Most of the people he knew were loggers like him. Two of his sisters and a brother were in high school in Budding, three other siblings still had grade school in Tesley, and the two youngest were still at home. At tenth grade, they either bussed or boarded out to Budding's high school. That's why he quit and went to work during tenth grade. He worked in a sawmill stacking lumber to start and boarded with his aunt and uncle in another town. He ran into some problems because he had a car and insurance but no driver's license. He had to leave his car where it was when he was stopped on the way to work one day. He walked the rest of the way to work but carried on using it afterward. Then he was a buckerman traveling from home to an hour out in the bush with his dad, who was a buckerman too. He liked that better, and the pay was better. He might be able to start another job skidding trees with the company's D6C Bulldozer Cat soon. His family had lived most of their life in Tesley. He knew almost everyone. He'd get his sisters to phone her and let her know when the next get together was. He had his driver's license now, so he'd take them to pick her up if she wanted. The town had a recreation community club that planned weekend outings.

Amber's parents were happy to see her being a part of the group of young people after their life-changing move to the Canadian wilderness small town. Truth be known, they had worried about her being an awkward loner, rarely dating. Only one young man, still a pen pal, had shown any lasting interest in her. So, when Marie, Sarah, or Alice (Cody's sisters) would phone with an invitation to go along with them on various outings, they encouraged her to go. Amber had planned only the summer with them before she would go back to the States for the quiet winter season to find work. They hoped she would be more outgoing when she started out to be on her own.

Tim came back to visit his parents in Tesley. He was an amateur guitar player and singer and planned a sing along around a campfire at Conifer Park. The campfire was burning brightly as Tim's close friends watched him take his guitar from its case to tune it up. Cody, his sisters, and Amber arrived. Soon Tim was leading the group of young people in popular country and Western songs. As the night wore on, most of the town's young people were gathered around the campfire. Norris and Clarence (seasonal forestry workers) decided the campfire needed rebuilding. Cody's sisters and Amber decided to use the woods instead of the smelly outhouse for their nature call while the fire was being built up. When they came back, Clarence was helping Norris roll the outhouse onto the campfire. Norris thought it would be funny to sit inside it until it began to burn in earnest. He escaped before burning himself. That was the first time the "pot" was ever smoked (and totally burnt up) in Tesley.

Forestry personnel saw the flames leaping up and came to check the park. The fire was put out, names were taken of all that were in attendance, and the sing-along ended. The next day, each youth was contacted to attend a park board meeting.

A community "kangaroo court" was held. A retired judge oversaw the proceedings. Each suspect was taken into a room where several members of the park board grilled them on how the outhouse got vandalized and burnt. Since Amber and Cody's sisters had accompanied each other in the woods, they were not really involved. However, by the preponderance of the other evidence gathered, the "court" sentenced Clarence and Norris to have a new outhouse built and installed in Conifer Park. Everyone who had attended the campfire were deemed "accessories" and sentenced to spend the next weekend in cleaning, repairing, and painting in the park. A fresh new outhouse hole was dug by hand as well as holes for the posts (to be painted) that sectioned off the play area. Small-town justice that turned out to be fun for the lesser offenders. After the work was completed, they headed for Flo's Cafe.

Locals, known by everyone as Uncle Ned and Aunty Rose, were there enjoying a meal out. The moccasin telegraph had been at work with its own version of events. "You're a bad little girl," Uncle Ned zeroed in on Amber as the group walked by them to a table of their own.

"Actually, us girls were using the woods for a bathroom break when everything was happening," Amber volunteered.

*Whack!* Aunty Rose hit Amber in her breast. "We don't believe that lie!"

*Well*, thought Amber as her face turned red with embarrassment, *I guess I'm a real part of the group now.*

Amber was fitting into the relaxed gatherings. Fishing, swimming, boating, hiking, and just sitting and sometimes singing around a campfire were Tesley's occupants' favorite pastimes. Many of the older teenagers were drinking beer, but not to excess, because a few members would not have allowed it. Cody's sister Alice phoned to invite Amber to watch a huge slash burn where a logged off area had been ignited to encourage healthy new growth and burn off the waste wood. Cody drove to pick Amber up by himself.

"Where are Sarah and Alice?" she asked. "Let's go get them." She was unaware that Cody had left them behind on purpose.

Cody had suffered from rejections of other girls who had dumped him for more popular, less primitive and more sophisticated, or wealthier boyfriends. He had used his sisters to get to know Amber in a group setting to protect his ego. He had planned to make a move toward claiming Amber as his girlfriend this night. Swallowing his disappointment, they went to pick up Sarah and Alice, who were always happy to have something interesting to do.

Cody drove up the twisting, rough backroads way up the mountain. As they drew nearer, the night sky was brightly flickering and glowing red with the fire. Glowing embers floated up to the stars lighting the entire hillside. It was an awesome sight. They could feel the heat and hear the dangerous roar of the fire snapping and crackling like a mythical monster. A complete mountain aglow was mesmerizing and kept them silently watching it.

Thinking of a commercial for a popular breakfast cereal, Amber quipped, "What do you get from forest fires?" Then, answering their questioning looks stated, "Crispy Critters!"

The unexpected pun made them all crack up laughing and broke the spell.

Cody pulled Amber close and explained how the old diseased, bug-ridden waste was burnt off safely to duplicate nature's way of creating a hearty new growth forest. The ground gets sterilized so the new growth has a healthier chance to resist bugs and diseases. The new trees that spring up again soon produce oxygen. It was also a way to discourage uncontrolled forest fires that happened in nature.

They could hear the thuds of falling pieces of trees. Amber had never seen anything that compared to it before. It was so fascinating to watch. Cody turned to watch her and impulsively kissed her. At first she drew away in panic and then made herself kiss back instead, not wanting to offend him. Cody was elated. He was sure there would be more kisses to come. She wasn't a girl to be rushed. There would be more times together without the constant chaperones she'd been so eager to keep around. He was glad he hadn't scared her off by moving too fast and made a mental note not to frighten the wide-eyed girl away by being too aggressive.

# Chapter 5

This was a whole new world to Amber. If she continued to put on a brave front with these woodsy (almost off the grid) small-town teens, they might not know how painfully awkward, shy, and insecure she always ended up feeling. They were used to outdoor plumbing, packing water, and old-style washing machines. Some had generator-powered light plants for electricity, and all had crank-operated party-line telephones…if they even had a phone. They lived wild and free, making do with what they had. They certainly weren't sophisticated and uppity but were friendly and accepting.

Her new friends had a fondness for the town gossip. They told how "Aunty Rose"—as everyone called her—"quit listening in and get off the phone" and was followed by an indignant "I'm not!" and a click of the receiver. "The overly endowed lady has quite a history," they eagerly told Amber. "She was a maid in a wealthy home where she got pregnant and gave the baby away. Then she met and married Uncle Ned while working in a logging camp that was out here. She never told him about the baby and they never had any children of their own. They used to babysit us whenever Mom was sick or having another baby. Sarah hid her dirtied underwear in Uncle Ned's toolbox once. You have got to watch Uncle Ned if you go to a dance if he's been drinking. His hands get a little too touchy feely! Aunty Rose loves to hug the boys between her extremely huge breasts so they can't even breathe. It's like being smothered by two huge pillows."

Amber didn't have to say much to keep the conversation flowing. They loved to tell her astonishing stories. All the newcomer had to say was, "Really?" or "You've got to be kidding. That is interesting and so funny!" Then a dozen more stories started up. There was a gold mine where miles of a huge mountain were washed away by gigantic hydraulic water pipes. A bunkhouse hotel housed some of the people working there. You can still see what's left of the hotel and the frames of some houses. Lots of Chinese workers were here, with their own style of homes. It's a good place to find antique Chinese pottery and bottles. Some of the huge pipe fittings are still around there too. There is a humungous hole where the water blasted away the top growth, soil, and rock to get at the gold, leaving a giant drop off. They even mined the tailings years later to get more gold recovery. Tourists still go there to look at what was done.

"I'd love to see all these things with you," was Amber's eager response.

Cody became Amber's knowledgeable guide to the area's history. Soon they were steadily dating by visiting many of the interesting sites.

Cody had brought three of his sisters and a little brother along when he invited Amber to go out with them to eat and see the trained monkey in the town's only cafe. Cody was funny and such a tease. It seemed everyone in the town knew and liked him. Stories flowed freely as the other customers acquainted Amber with more of the town's background. Flo and Hank had once cooked at a lodge that catered to wealthy city folks looking for a wild wilderness experience. (The lodge was nestled just up the valley surrounded by mountains, next to the huge, deep pristine lake. Fishing was great and wildlife was abundant.)

Flo was a salty character who didn't give two bits if her customers were paying for their meals anyhow. If she cooked it for them, they were expected to eat all of it, or she'd better know why! Hank jumped to every expected task with nervous energy (causing some of the locals to label him as Flo's "trained monkey"). Flo ran the show, but if everything was caught up, Hank would launch into outlandish tales of his past. He was the hero who nearly single-handedly had blown a hillside up to change the course of a river to create the lake. He had traveled the earth and seen and done amazing things (like many people recognized as having read about in the *National*

*Geographic* magazine), he claimed as his own experience. They were real to him and entertaining to his audiences, even if he had to be well over one hundred years old to have done some of the things he described. Hank's greatest pride though was in his Flo. Big and gruff as she seemed, Flo oozed with love for her wiry little husband. She mothered each of her customers whether she felt they needed scolding or encouragement.

What surprised and shocked Amber was how those around them were saying "Jesus Christ" and "Goddamn Almighty" as part of every other sentence. Maybe this was a very religious town indeed! She'd been taught to respect those names. You'd better know what you were asking for if you asked God to damn something instead of His blessing for it. All those four letter words, she believed to be vulgar foul language, were just part of their normal talk. Wow! Even children, barely learning to speak (like Cody's youngest brother and sister), spoke rougher than anyone Amber had known before. Cody saw her eyes widen at some conversations and was glad he had been curbing his tongue around her.

Amber was impressed when Cody paid for his whole table's meals as if it was just his habit to be generous. He refused her offer to help pay, explaining that he was the only one with a regular paycheck. She was used to paying her own way in groups but thanked him instead of continuing to argue.

# Chapter 6

"Tingly...my wrists feel hot like the blood is rushing through them." Amber sounded breathless. For their good-night kiss, Cody had gathered her up in his strong arms against his tall frame to lift her off her feet. He let her slide down his lean body's arousal to touch the ground. He smiled a bit smugly down at her as she gazed startled and innocently up at him. "I'd better go, good night," she said shakily, embarrassed by her honest admission.

Cody had already asked Amber to go steady. Despite her refusal (saying they didn't know each other well enough), they were dating only each other. Since she was the new girl in Tesley, where most of the other girls were his sisters, his friends recognized his claim to her. Amber still wrote her childhood pen pal and hadn't told him she had a boyfriend either. Andrew wanted to come for a visit to see her again, and her parents were encouraging it. The town's tendency for heavy drinking made them wary of Amber's growing relationship with Cody. Amber had found a job at Tesley's general store, so she wasn't moving back to the States.

Cody was in his element showing Amber around. He had gone moose and deer hunting down almost every backroad around Tesley. He had a great memory for all the places within driving distance and the histories behind them. It was just natural for him to drive Amber out to see these unique, now abandoned places. He loved the outdoors, grown up exploring and utilizing it, going fishing and hunting, and he showed it well, capturing Amber's interest. The rough gravel roads were only an opportunity to swerve at the right moment to jostle Amber closer to him. Each touch energized their excitement with each other. Then, the good-night kiss and Cody's hands began to roam.

As she grew up, Amber had become a firm believer that if she were a "good girl," all those sexual feelings should not be explored until after marriage. When she resisted, Cody backed off, only to try again later. He recognized her body's response. He loved that she wasn't "easy," but he wanted more. At first she shoved his hands back off her breasts. Cody would continue to kiss and neck with her, giving her, her first hickey. She was giving in to the heated craving to be caressed and fondled. He gently took her hands and encouraged her to stroke his lean muscular body, even if she wouldn't touch below the belt.

"Marry me, marry me, sweetheart," Cody began to urge Amber. "We love each other. We'll get married. Start our own family." Surely those were honorable intentions.

Amber's parents had always taught her to go to God and read what the Bible said if she was unsure of her choices. Her parents still held hands and kissed, showing love and attraction for each other, as well as love for family and friends. Amber prayed for direction. Marriage had to be for keeps and lifestyle would be important. "Don't be unequally yoked…" the Bible cautioned her. "Song of Solomon" in the Old Testament enticed her with physical delights it described (like "under her tongue are…" in chapter 7).

"Do you believe in God?" Amber asked Cody after still unsure how to answer his continuing marriage proposals. She knew Cody had a very different upbringing than she had. He had been smoking and drinking since childhood. His peers were proud to be "rednecks." He could treat people with honesty and respect and then rudely curse them and accuse them unfairly in the next breathe. Easy to like, friendly and funny, he still had a bad, uncontrollable temper with built in mistrust of others. She had occasionally been shocked with the thundering loud foul language he used when he was angry with someone. He certainly was a dyed in the wool redneck.

Cody considered her question. "There were people who came here when I was a kid and held Sunday school once a month in the school house. They taught us about God loving us. Yeah…I believe in God," he answered, knowing what Amber would want to hear.

This wild boy-man often drank heavily with his friends. He was usually a happy drunk, promising to make Amber his queen. He wanted her for his own like she had never been wanted before. She did so want to belong somewhere, to someone. She loved him too, but was it enough for a lifetime? Were they both sure? Her mind warned her to be careful, but her body begged her to do what was necessary to give in to the desires that were burning more and more insistently.

"Yes, we'll get married," she agreed. She hoped Andrew only thought of her as a friend when she wrote to tell him she was going to be married but was still hoping he would be able to come to visit in Tesley. She and her parents would love to see him. Andrew never wrote back again.

"We're getting married because we love each other, not because we have to, like Sandy, the bitch slut, trapped Eric." (Sandy was an old girlfriend that had dumped Cody for more sophisticated, playboy Eric). "We'll have a big wedding in Spring with all our brothers and sisters part of it. We can plan it right away and start looking for a place to live!" Cody said proudly.

"My sister Andrea still lives in the States and won't be able to get here for our wedding until she finishes college and then immigrates for their jobs in Fort St. John with her family. Late summer would be better. She has to be part of our wedding too!" Amber insisted.

Reluctantly Cody agreed. He angrily remembered the time he'd told an old-school friend of his and his sister Alice, to stay away from Amber because she was his. Amber found out and stubbornly still visited with his sister and her friends. "You don't own me!" she'd defiantly said when he called her a traitorous bitch. He would wait, but she would be his and he would be in control then!

Cody experimented in their necking sessions by purposely arousing Amber, then backing off. The more reserve he practiced, the more receptive Amber seemed to become to his advances the next time. His hands knew the upper part of her body quite well and her stifled moans betrayed her desire for more. He'd wait to be married alright, but he'd be having her before then. The girl seemed chaste, but he'd started her fire and knew it.

They told their parents of their plans to marry. Though Amber's parents had their reservations about the match, they thought the timeframe of waiting for Andrea's freedom to attend would be a good waiting period. Gert prepared a get to know each other dinner with Cody and his parents. Two very different backgrounds, but both sets of parents pleasantly spent the evening getting acquainted. They all showed their loving support toward the future couple.

Amber was surprised at the gift Cody gave her on her birthday. A large stuffed teddy bear instead of a ring. Subconsciously he was waiting for her to give herself to him before he gave her an engagement ring. He knew women could never really be trusted. Though their time together was spent talking and necking, Cody was getting more aggressive. "We're getting married. If you really loved me, you would let me," he reasoned.

As their passion gained more and more control, Amber would declare in return, "If you really loved me, you would want to protect me by waiting for our marriage. Remember what you told me about your old girlfriend. I remember how you called me 'Samber' when you started to call me by Sandy's name, but I'm not like her at all!"

Cody referred to Sandy as a slut, whore, bitch who purposely trapped her new boyfriend into marrying her by getting pregnant to get what she wanted. Often Cody referred to other women with derisive names, showing what lack of respect he was capable of toward women. Though Amber was wary, she had forgiven him for the time he had called her down.

Mostly she thought of his quick sense of humor, his riotous laugh that caused others to laugh at his jokes even if his jokes were totally unfunny. "Your teeth are like the stars… They come out at night," or "Your eyes are shimmering…like cesspools," would crack Cody up laughing until tears came to his eyes. He thought it was funny to blow a loud fart and blame it on her. Even if Amber was shocked or angry, she'd end up laughing with him.

When their bodies finally joined, Amber reasoned with herself that they were going to get married. They had already made a commitment to each other. Still, she felt ashamed.

Cody's friends were fond of Amber and asked why she still didn't have an engagement ring. She blushed, hoping they didn't know how intimate they had occasionally become.

"I'd have a ring on your finger if you were my girl!" Jim said. "Don't know what you're waiting for." He looked at Cody and shrugged.

Right around the time Cody had wanted to get married, he gave Amber an engagement ring. He made sure Jim saw it on her finger.

A subtle change came into their relationship. Cody was no longer content to talk for hours and spend most of his free time with Amber. He expected her body to respond to his advances even as he talked more about other women being sluts and whores. His drinking and partying with his buddies increased. Amber expressed her concern about marriage to someone who drank so much and spent his money partying.

"I'll quit if you want me to," Cody promised. "I love you, sweetheart. I'll never have another drink if that's what you want. I'm going to make you my queen! You won't work when we're married. I'll bring home the bacon. You'll just cook it."

Knowing it was a promise destined to be broken, as well as his dislike of bossy women, Amber replied, "You don't have to never drink. Just control it. Don't let it control you. But please don't drink on our wedding day, okay?" She tried to be understanding. Cody cut back for a few days.

## Chapter 7

"Don't be a stick in the mud! Everyone drinks here! It's just harmless fun. Loosen up a little," Cody urged Amber to drink. They went to house parties and to community hall dances. Amber soon found out it was fine for Cody to enjoy his friends and mingle and dance with other women, but she'd better not dance or talk too much with men who started a conversation with her. At first it was sure to get his attention. He'd pull her to himself, away from others. Then he'd often find an isolated spot to leave her again. Her awkward shyness kept her from circulating unless someone approached her first. Cody seemed to have no interest in making her feel at ease.

A gentleman sat down by Amber and began a conversation. He escorted her onto the dance floor when she consented to dance with him. He complimented her and thanked her for the dance as Cody's buddy, Freddy, came up to them. Freddy was cutting it up, trying to get her to dance with him. The gentleman grinned and left.

Freddy started dancing alone in front of Amber until she tried to follow his dance moves with a bit more grace. She noticed Cody dancing with an old girlfriend. Sally's bosom was pushed up in her low cleavage and her body was pressed tightly against him. Her short mini skirt almost showed her underwear. Sally was moving suggestively, giving Amber a smug look. Amber was grateful for Freddy's diversion and laughed as she followed his leads.

After the dance, Cody walked over and grabbed Amber's arm. "Let's go!" There was anger, pleading, and command in his voice. She nodded, gave her thanks to Freddy, and left with Cody. He steered her to his car, opening the driver's side indicating for her to get in first.

He got in beside her and pulled her into a rough kiss. Then he drove quickly to a dark quiet side road, parked, and turned off his car.

"What's going on?" Amber tried to ask.

"Don't!" Cody shook his head. "Don't!" He shuddered. His face was a mask of torment and anger. He gripped the steering wheel until his knuckles went white.

Amber could feel herself shrinking away from him. All kinds of thoughts and emotions were tearing at them both. Amber was wondering if he was still holding a torch for Sally and she was just second choice or what.

Cody glanced sideways at Amber's troubled eyes gazing into the dark. He both wanted to protect her from being hurt and wanted to really hurt her because of the mistrust of women that overwhelmed him. His hands moved to grip the steering column as if it was someone's neck. "I love you. Oh, God, can I trust you?" he forced out. "Can I trust you?" His hands could easily choke her to death, he thought, if he couldn't trust her. If he couldn't keep her, no one else would get to have her. Sally had tempted him and told him how unhappy she was. What a good friend he'd always been. He was the only one who'd tried to make her happy and everyone else only cared about themselves. He was the only one who cared if she lived or died, the only one who wanted her for who she really truly was.

At first Cody had swelled with pride and temptation. Sexy Sally wanted him back! As she gyrated against him, he saw his buddy Freddy being a funny drunk clown. Amber was on the dance floor with him, shyly indulgent, trying to play along with his antics gracefully. Suddenly Sally's words meant nothing to him. Her pressing body repelled him. The dance was over none too soon for both of them. Sally set out for another partner the moment she realized Cody's eyes and thoughts were on Amber, not her.

"*Ooohhh*, there's Ralphy." She simpered. "He always told me I was the hottest thing in skirts or pants!" Cody was already walking away toward Amber.

"The steering wheel can't breathe. You've choked it to death…" a quiet voice broke through his trance. Amber recognized Cody's potential for violence, his need for someone to love and trust. She wanted to be there for him.

Cody's hands jumped of their own accord to Amber's throat. They stroked it gently as his lips caressed her. Then he held her tight with her head against his chest and his chin on her head. They clung together while their pulses raced. Their minds and bodies calmed. The night air cooled the car and they awoke looking into each other's eyes.

"You have beautiful bedroom eyes!" Cody kissed her passionately.

"You have a one-track mind," Amber retorted with a laugh. She wistfully thought how it would be to wake up this way for countless days to come, without the shame that inhibited her to indulge in the passion she craved. *God created sexuality,* she thought defiantly. Then, involuntary the thought followed, *He also created marriage to protect His precious gift.* "We'll be married soon," she said aloud.

"We'd be married now if it wasn't for your sister," Cody attempted to reason with her. "It's only a piece of paper."

"You're the one who said we were getting married because we loved each other, not because I get pregnant," Amber said without conviction.

Cody sighed, started his car, and drove Amber home. "Was she actually stubborn and brave enough not to go ahead with their marriage if he lost control too often? He had to maintain control or she could, like now, make him afraid that he could still lose her. He couldn't let himself want or trust her too much. She'd better make up her mind once and for all if she was his or not. He'd need to be the first to pull away at all cost. He couldn't want her more than she wanted him. She was shy enough to depend on him in a crowd, but he didn't need a clinging vine to cramp his freedom either. She wasn't a raving beauty that other guys were tripping over. Some of them were taking a second look, especially when she got dressed up. Her face did light up with a smile that reached her eyes. Those eyes! Sometimes they flashed fire, and sometimes he had to fight not to be influenced by their passion or hurt. Her wide-eyed innocence makes even Freddy want to protect her. She's not real smart or witty either. She cares and listens though. A lot of people open up to her about what they'd tell no one else. She's unsure of herself. Yeah! She's unsure of herself. She might be more educated and school smart, but he was quicker and smart where it counted. He was more comfortable around others. She almost seemed scared in a crowd if she wasn't with someone." Cody's thoughts rambled through his mind.

"You've never seen the lakeshore ten miles up, have you?" Cody offered. "We could go camping with the group of us for the weekend. It's kind of a tradition. We take a pot luck bunch of food with us. We'd be chaperoned. Freddy and I have a couple tents with room for my sisters and us. My parents and lots of their friends are going too. I'll buy you some of the brandy you like the taste of. It really is beautiful this time of year. There is a waterfall they call 'Little Niagara'…" His voice trailed off.

Amber nodded. "Sure, it would be great to see how you brave the wilderness. I love it when you share your love of nature with me." Silently she thought, "Maybe it will ease this emotional tension, to go where he can teach me more about this untamed land." Aloud she added, "I'll try not to be a stick in the mud." She knew alcohol was a big part of the potluck. Many preachers had extolled the wickedness of alcohol, but her parents had never condemned it. She'd never seen a drunk person in her sheltered life on their dairy farm. A sip of wine mixed with hot water to ease a fever, or a beer to quench the thirst after a sweltering day of hay harvest was quite acceptable moderation. Aside from that, it helped to make her more comfortable in this group of people who were so much a part of Cody's life. She would make the effort to lighten up and just have fun. Abstinence could control a person as well as overindulgence.

Cody, Freddy, Sarah, and Alice came to pick up Amber for the weekend, already drinking, smiling, and joking together. (In Tesley, any teenager could drink and smoke. Cody had started smoking, even with adult encouragement and approval, way younger. It was their redneck way of life.) The group looked forward to enjoying themselves without a care in the world.

"Here's the brandy I bought for you, Amber." Cody laid his arm warmly over her shoulder as he drove with an opened beer between his legs. Soon they were bouncing down the winding, muddy road to the beach. When they arrived, they scrambled out and unloaded their supplies. The tents were quickly set up. With ice chests of food and surely more alcohol than would ever be drank in one weekend, the camping out began. Soon a nice campfire was burning brightly. True to form, Amber sat as close to Cody as he pulled her.

He was having one beer after another, laughing at the good-natured teasing about bringing along the "ball and chain" with him. The look he gave Amber spoke volumes as he tipped back his beers. He didn't want her to say one word about how much he was drinking. He took a big slug of the brandy. "Have some more brandy. Don't you like what I got for you?" he gruffly said. "Don't be such a stick in the mud again!"

Amber sipped and smiled shyly. "It's very delicious, but it makes me a bit tipsy." She was trying to fit in, though, by pretending to be drinking more than she was actually swallowing.

One of the ladies began telling Amber how her potato salad was praised at every camp out. She told her the secret ingredients. They were chatting comfortably and enjoying the comradery.

Suddenly Cody abruptly got up. "Stop clinging to me!" he ordered as he went for more beer.

Amber was shocked and embarrassed. She chatted for a while longer, but when the campfire circle broke up to begin dinner preparations, she got up also. She added her contributions to the makeshift tables and then went to answer a nature call.

When she returned, everyone was busily paired off in groups. Cody glanced at her from a group of men who were laughing loudly. Then he turned back to say something that made them howl with laughter again. Some of the men looked at Amber and nodded, but Cody avoided looking at her again.

Amber looked around the scene. It really was so beautiful. She picked up the abandoned brandy, took a stiff swallow, and placed it beside their tent. Then she went for a walk to explore the beach and paths that she found. Unique pieces of driftwood lined the shore. Ferns and wildflowers pushed through the moss carpet in the path leading through the woods. Squirrels scolded and chattered at her as they ran about the woods. Birds serenaded her as she walked. A startled deer ran to hide. She heard the waterfall and felt the mist before the path opened up to the exceptional view. Water spilled through the mountain gorge, nothing short of spectacular. A huge, pointed rock reached toward the sky to divide the water as it rushed toward the lake. The sun created a glorious rainbow through the waterfall's mist. As Amber climbed gingerly around the slippery large boulders, she was fascinated by the round circular pools worn into the wet surfaces by years of smaller rocks and swirling water wearing away inside seemingly solid rocks. Finally, she tore herself away from the amazing scene. She started back down the path. It hadn't seemed as long going up as it did going back, but she was quite sure it was the same path. A rustling noise, away in the trees, was coming closer and making her feel uneasy. She hoped the sun wasn't starting to go down. With relief, she saw the glow of the campfire in the distance. She had just started off the path and was walking across the beach toward the main group when Cody spotted her.

He quickly walked toward her. "Where were you? I was worried about you," he said as he gathered her in his strong arms.

"I went for a walk. It was beautiful by the waterfall. I could hardly tear myself away," she explained.

"You shouldn't do that by yourself. You could get lost, run into a bear or cougar, or fall and get hurt. I couldn't stand it if something were to happen to you!" Cody seemed genuinely concerned. Unknown to Amber, he was worried that she'd overheard or guessed how he'd been bragging about how much of the upper hand he had in their relationship. No ball and chain there, he could do what he wanted and that little lady would be there to fall all over him whenever and wherever he wanted. Maybe he should make her barefoot and pregnant. She'd still aim to please him because she wasn't the most beautiful or smartest, but she seemed faithful at least. A guy had a better chance if other guys weren't after his bitch. When he realized what he was saying, even through his alcohol blur, he was ashamed. To save face, he hadn't obviously gone to look for Amber. However, he kept a furtive outlook hoping to spot her. He drank more slowly and sobered slightly.

He was so obviously relieved to see her that Amber enjoyed the idea that he was truly concerned and protective of her. She responded warmly to his kiss. He led her to dish up their picnic dinner and then motioned to where they could sit together. After eating the food, Cody was almost sober again.

"Here," he said, "I found your brandy by the tent when I looked to see if you were there. Have some, and stay closer to me now, you hear!" He winked and squeezed her hand.

Everyone was just having fun, joking, laughing, fondly enjoying each other's company. The brandy tasted wonderful out in the fresh air, sitting by the campfire with Cody's arm protectively around her.

"This'll be." Amber giggled at the way her words slurred and tried again. "This…will…be…a night to remember." She put the lid back on the brandy and contentedly watched the goings on around her. Freddy was sitting close to Sarah and talking quietly. Alice had gone to the tent for a quick nap to get ready to stay up later.

Amber stifled a yawn. "You're not going to be party pooper and want to go to sleep already too, are you?" Cody teased. "Have a little more brandy. Look! Old George is getting ready to sing and play the spoons. He sings when he's feeling good and keeps time by tapping two spoons in his hand like this." Cody showed her how the spoons held upside down against each other with a finger in between could be made to clack in rhythm by tapping against his leg and her leg while his other hand caught the bounce on the way up. Amber gave it a try and made it work before she gave the spoons back to Cody.

"You've sure got rhythm, real good rhythm, baby!" Amber laughed as Cody kept playing the spoons. She sipped more brandy.

George sang good old country songs, making up his own words for lines he forgot. He kept rhythm with the spoons and nodded his appreciation for Cody's accompaniment. "This is for you two," he said as he sang Charley Pride's "You've got to kiss an angel good morning and tell her that you love her all day long." When he noticed Cody put his spoons down, he said, "Keep playing. You're doing great." He gave Amber a roguish wink.

"You're doing fine by yourself." Cody smiled. He put his arm around Amber as George grinned knowingly. It was clear that George and others were just getting started, winding up to party for hours. Alice had rejoined the party also.

"I've got to go for a nature call," Cody told Amber after a couple more hours of the campfire entertainment. "Maybe we should turn in for the night after."

Amber agreed. She felt quite tipsy but managed to walk and answer her own nature call without swaying. The tent was empty, so she quickly got ready to crawl into her sleeping bag. Cody came inside, undressed, and crawled into his sleeping bag. He embraced and kissed Amber until she moaned with passion. Her head felt cloudy, but her body never felt more unsatisfied with his gentle caressing. Cody shushed her.

"I want you," she whispered, almost pleading. What could Cody do but as quietly as possible oblige. He was back into his own sleeping bag, and Amber was already asleep when Freddy and Sarah's flashlight lit up the outside of the tent. Sarah crawled inside to bed for the night, but Freddy went back to the campfire. Cody could hear Freddy singing with George as he fell asleep next to his future wife.

# Chapter 8

Cody and Amber soon began looking for houses that would be reasonable enough to buy. Indoor plumbing was a priority to Amber. They found a small house and acreage touching the riverside with a view of the lake. Amber's parents generously loaned them the money (from their hard-earned nest egg) for a down payment. The owners agreed to take monthly payments for the balance they would owe. They began shopping for secondhand furnishings. It didn't matter to them if nothing was new if it meant they could move into their own home after their marriage. Cody proudly parked his antique car in the yard and only drove his newer car. They diligently began making payments on loan and home.

All of Cody's and Amber's sisters and brothers (with their mates) were going to be part of their wedding party. His buddy, Freddy, to be the best man, and sister Sarah, the maid of honor. Amber bought yards of material from her savings. She designed the bridesmaids' dresses and her wedding gown and veil after pouring through bridal magazines for ideas. Then she began sewing on the treadle sewing machine her mother gave her to keep. Her white satin dress was a sleeveless sheath to the floor with a full lace covering over top and slim lace sleeves coming to a triangular point just past her wrists. She taped a cardboard halo shaped crown together to fit her head and then covered it with satin and lace. She attached netting so it flowed from the center of the crown to form the train. She made all the bridesmaid dresses in a short sheath design in a soft lilac color and the flower girl's to match. A matching short netted veil was fashioned for each by sewing it onto a hair clip by hand, covering the clip with a bit of their dress material. The girls seemed pleased with the final look. Cody and the men arranged to rent their suits. Such a large wedding party could have been too expensive without the personal involvement.

Amber's family and friends insisted that she need not worry at all about the wedding reception. They arranged to rent Tesley's community hall. They prepared all the decorations, food, drinks, and even the wedding cake themselves. Most of the town would be coming to the reception and many helped with the preparations in the close knit community. Some of Amber's and Cody's aunts and uncles reserved cabins for the event at her parents resort.

The marriage itself would be held in Budding, as no one in Tesley could legally perform a marriage. Cody and Amber had the necessary meetings with the pastor who would perform the ceremony. His counseling session ended with him giving them material to read that would "point them in the right direction so the love they had now would only be a beginning for the love their future would hold."

Everyone took time from their busy lives to practice the wedding procession. The whirl of activity and preparation still allowed Amber to realize her period was a month late. She was terribly ashamed to know she had to be pregnant (birth control wasn't used by people who planned to wait until they were married). *So much for getting married because we don't have to,* she thought grimly in a moment of self-reproach. Soon after she told Cody that she might be pregnant, their wedding day arrived.

Amber and her sisters traveled with her parents over the long, winding gravel road to Budding early in the morning. Her sister, Andrea, became carsick and their mother looked like she was turning green also. "I'm so sorry," Andrea apologized profusely, "and on your wedding day too!"

"It's not like you're sick on purpose," Amber tried to reassure her. "You'll feel better after we get off this dusty, winding road… Go ahead, have my wedding jitters for me. I'm still calm and doing fine."

They arrived at their reserved motel rooms in Budding excited but glad that the wedding day had arrived. All the girls were in a flurry of getting dressed and looking in the mirrors. Soon the men were together in their own room, also getting ready, before all meeting at the church.

Amber's father looked handsome and proud as he escorted her up the aisle to where the rest of the wedding party waited.

"Who gives this woman to be married to this man?" the pastor asked as they approached.

"Her mother and I," her father replied as he released his young daughter. Then he sat next to his own bride of thirty years.

Traditional vows and rings were exchanged. "You may kiss the bride." Then off to the side room to sign the marriage license while the organ music played and the ring bearer and flower girl played catch with the ring pillow.

"Ladies and gentlemen, I present to you"—pause—"Mr. and Mrs. Cody Bentley!" The organ music thundered as Cody and Amber walked through the aisle of the church as man and wife. Unruly young guests crowded behind them.

Instead of being able to form a proper reception line, they were swarmed and being pounded on the back, kissed, and congratulated. They were crowded outside while rice and confetti rained down on them. Freddy and Sarah had Cody's car parked with the back door open to take them to the photographer's shop. Soon both sets of parents and the wedding party joined them there. Black and white pictures would fill an album that would end with Cody kissing Amber. A black key-shaped cover surrounded the kiss. It represented their journey behind a closed door that others could only peak at through the keyhole.

They drove back to Tesley for the wedding reception in Cody's car with Freddy at the wheel and Sarah beside him. Freddy had had a few quick beer in between best man duties. "Had to make Cody have a beer to settle him down for the wedding. He was a nervous wreck!" he informed Amber. "Just one though."

*So,* thought Amber, *Cody had tried to keep his promise not to drink before their ceremony on their wedding day.* She was proud of him for that.

Freddy was normally a good driver but had there been a police road check, he would have been well over the alcohol limit—and the speed limit. He swerved recklessly at a roadside cow in a show of bravado and went into a skid on the loose gravel.

"Watch it, man," Cody, next to Amber, growled from the back seat. "We'd like to get our honeymoon in before you kill us." Freddy slowed down and paid better attention.

As soon as they reached Tesley, honking horns greeted them, so they drove down main street, back up past the hall, down to Conifer Park, and back to the hall with a celebratory procession of well-wishers. They greeted their guests at the town hall. It had been transformed by lovely decorations. Paper wedding bells and streamers were everywhere. A huge banner with a big heart proclaimed "*Cody and Amber Bentley.*" Everyone laughed and enjoyed themselves through the toasts and jokes, dinner, and cake cutting.

Cody's head fit above Amber's as he led his bride in their wedding dance. For a brief moment she laid her head against his chest and there was just the two of them. Then a swirl of partners, good-natured advice, warnings, and professed broken hearts. Time raced.

Amber threw her bouquet and Sarah caught it. Cody and she thanked everyone and got ready to leave for their honeymoon. They waved and hugged their goodbyes and then left in Cody's now decorated car.

# Chapter 9

It wasn't long before they discovered that the horn honked each time the lights were lowered for other traffic. Amber's brother was a handy mechanic. They could picture him grinning in anticipation of his practical joke. They had planned a cross country road trip to the beautiful Lake Louise, Jasper and Calgary. Both exhausted, they stopped at the first motel they came to.

"We're married," Cody told the unconcerned desk clerk who had only a two-twin-bed room to rent to them. They took the room.

They were both unexpectedly shy as they prepared for bed. Amber climbed into one of the beds in her sheer flowing nightgown. "You can't be a chicken all your life," Cody said with a boyish grin as he came over to share her bed. Their marriage was consummated quickly, no longer a reason to deny their passion. A short night's sleep in the uncomfortable bed and Cody became poetic. "Once a king, always a king—once a knight is enough." He grinned at his bride as he lied to her.

Amber was surprised that she missed the foreplay Cody had used when he'd stoked her desire in order to overcome her "good girl" morals. No matter how many times they came together, she was left wanting more when Cody quickly climaxed. Cody wondered at how Amber's "No, we shouldn't, we can't" had changed to "Let's do it again." He didn't know her body craved a climax. He had no idea his quickened response took her body longer to reach. Amber couldn't put into words that her body was at the peak of desire when he was already spent. She blushed to think that he'd also be embarrassed if she were to blurt, "Please touch and caress my body like you used to before. My breasts feel neglected." Instead her eagerness kept Cody from waiting and kept her thinking, "This time it will be like it was when I was out of my head wanting him." They were both inexperienced in the art of love making.

"Marriage has sure changed your appetite for sex!" Cody was trying to understand how wrong she could think it was before and how ready and willing she was now.

"We belong to each other now," Amber tried to explain.

Cody had no problem acknowledging that Amber was his and had he his own way, would have been his from the moment he wanted her. That she was now claiming him was a bit much. He was his own man! He was the boss who had the upper hand, not her. She'd better learn that it was his needs she had to meet. She wasn't going to get what she wanted from him by controlling him, even by using sex. His parents had a good marriage. His dad was the boss and bread winner. His mom seemed content to take care of her large family. He'd often heard his father, Calvin, and his close friend Arnold discussing how some women ruled their men.

"Why a man can't even enjoy what he works for before their wives spend it…or they end up leaving them and taking everything they can get ahold of. Barefoot and pregnant," advised childless Arnold, "that's the way to keep them. Never let them get the upper hand. When I tell my Esther to do anything at all, she does it! Cooking and cleaning and looking after her man and family. That's her job! Give an inch, they'll take a mile. When I get home from work, my Esther undoes my boots and brings me a drink or two before dinner like she should. If a woman doesn't know her place, it's up to her man to make her know it."

*Of course,* Cody thought, *when Mom had been sick, Dad had taken care of her and didn't worry about being the boss again until she was better. She made do with what they had and didn't nag about what they didn't have. Fighting and drinking was just a part of life. Good times and partying and drinking were more important than having a fancy home with indoor plumbing and extra conveniences for the women who only looked after their home and family. Money was meant to be spent, not saved for the future. So what if Amber's father hadn't wasted any time in starting to build Gert a big house with indoor plumbing and a good heating system. Maybe she wasn't as really hardworking as she seemed but was just another spoiled wife. Their little house had indoor plumbing and a wood heater already, so Amber better appreciate it and not expect more changes to be made!*

Amber was looking through the envelope of money that had been taken up for them to use on their honeymoon. Cody grabbed it away. "We'll go shopping and go get something to eat," he decided.

They had a filling lunch at a small cafe and then went shopping. Amber encouraged Cody to get the clothes he found for himself. She really didn't need anything for herself, knowing money was limited. She would love to go to the museum though.

"You could just read about the museum," Cody stated. "We really don't know our way around and I'm not used to driving in all this traffic."

"I noticed"—Amber giggled—"when you stopped to wait for a car that was three blocks away before you pulled out into it."

"He was only one block away!" Cody grinned with a sheepish twinkle in his eyes. "You could drive better you think?" He pretended to be hurt.

"We almost got a divorce the last time you were tired and got me to drive. You yelled at me because you didn't think I was doing it right." Amber laughed. "No, thanks, you really like to be the one at the wheel."

"I wasn't putting you down. I was just trying to make you better at some of what you do again," Cody stated.

Cody was walking ahead along the sidewalk, as Amber seemed to take two steps to his long legged one step. She caught up to him, putting her hand on his arm. She thought of walking hand in hand as her parents would. He immediately pulled away with a disgusted look.

"Don't hang on me. People will look!" he grumbled.

"So what if they do? What's the harm in holding hands as if we at least like each other?" Amber felt rejected. Already she knew better than to argue with him once he made up his mind. He was showing the hot tempered side of himself that she'd been shocked to see him use on his sisters if they crossed him. "People he grew up with were rough around the edges," she reminded herself. When she sighed, Cody responded in profanity. He strode ahead and waited for her in the car.

Once they were traveling again, Amber tried not to invade Cody's space. She was enjoying and occasionally commenting on the beautiful scenery. Cody pulled her closer. A pattern was beginning to form. As long as Amber strove for closeness, Cody was aloof. When she showed an interest outside of him, he wanted her attention back and usually got it.

Cody could spot an animal, usually camouflaged by its surroundings, so often that Amber was awed. He basked in her pleasure when he pointed them out to her. Years of hunting had given him a practiced eye for spotting deer, moose, and other animals while still keeping an eye on the road. He only hunted for food, yet he loved just watching wild animals every bit as much. Occasionally he would pull safely to the side of the road just so they could watch them. Love of nature was a strong bond between them. Cody had grown up familiar with the untamed wilderness, so Amber became his admiring student. He enjoyed sharing his knowledge (which had seemed just like common sense to him) with an appreciative audience.

"I'll take you hunting with us," Cody promised, "but you've got to be careful where and how you walk, not to make any noise or talk and spook the deer or moose. I'll show you!" He could picture her following him through the deep woods. He'd silently point out tracks made by moose, deer, wolves, cougars, or even rabbits. He could recognize them all and show her the difference. After he scanned the area, he'd be able to show her where the deer or moose bit off tender young willow shoots as they grazed. Amber would be so proud of the meat he'd provide for his family. She didn't look pregnant. He was proud of the baby growing inside of her. His father would be proud of him if it were a boy first. No one was going to call any of his children bastards like they'd called him! He loved babies, a girl would be fine too, but a man needed a son to carry on the family name. They would go hunting and fishing together. His children would get a good education, finish high school for sure, and maybe go to college even. He would teach them things they wouldn't learn in schools. They wouldn't quit school and go to work at fifteen like he did, though. Amber was school smart, but he was much smarter than her really. His children would still get their education because he would provide it.

"Penny for your thoughts," Amber's voice caressed him.

"Let's find a campsite, my wife." Cody eyed her up and down. "You don't need to unpack anything but the sleeping bags while I get the tent and heavy things." He felt protective of her.

Amber blushed as she remembered her aggressive actions in another tent. Cody pulled into an isolated campsite. There was a calm lake where ducks swam about, and an elk raised its majestic head, where it was taking a drink, to look at them. It walked regally away with its head held high. A fish jumped, leaving ripples in the water out past the rickety dock.

After setting up camp, Cody put his arm around Amber, who was watching the scene before them. They leaned into each other and caught up in the moment. He kissed her hair, nibbled her ear, and tenderly kissed her neck. Still keeping one arm around her, he gently guided her into the tent. Amber felt dizzy and weak kneed. They dropped to the sleeping bags after slowly and deliciously undressing each other. A squirrel scolded noisily outside.

Cody lay on his stomach and kissed and stroked Amber until she was quietly moaning in pleasure. "Do you want me?" he teased. "Are you sure it's okay now? I love you, my darling wife. I love you, my bride."

"I love you!" Amber responded. "So much, so good…sooo good, mmmhhm." Afterward, Amber's eyes filled with tears.

"What's wrong, lover?" Cody thought of the baby, ready to panic, concerned if their intensity had caused problems.

Amber shook her head, trying to get her voice. "Do you love me really? Really? I'm so scared sometimes, what it would be like if you didn't love me back. You have way too much power over me… Hold me, please hold me."

Cody held her. She fell asleep as he gently rubbed her back and wiped away her tears. "Strange, horny little monkey," he whispered. He slept a little uncomfortably with the bundle in his strong arms.

The squirrel scolded with renewed vigor. Amber shifted in her sleep, waking Cody.

He went outside to the lake and contemplated how to catch a fish. He cut a willow stick for the line and hook he had in the glove box of the car. He'd caught one fish and was trying for another when he noticed Amber looking from him to the fish.

"Come here, I'll show you how to catch a fish on a willow stick," Cody offered.

"You don't even have a rod and reel. You're just teasing me," Amber challenged.

"Hold it like this," Cody instructed. "Keep the tip up. Hold the line here and then let it go as you sling the line way out with the baited hook… Okay, try again."

"I'll humor you"—Amber grinned—"but I can't believe you can catch a fish this way!" But she did, squealing with delight as she dragged it to shore.

"Now what do you think about your big strong Daniel Boon? I'll show you how to survive in the wilderness," Cody drawled. He was pleased to see that Amber's was the bigger fish.

"I think he must be a keeper, you and the fish." Amber winked. "I might just follow you wherever you take me!"

"What?" Cody razzed her. "You want me to take you again? There's only so much nagging and demands a man can put up with! He can't do everything you want all the time!" He came toward her as if ready to go back into the tent with her.

"Go ahead, clean our fish then." She ducked and played along. "I'll just get the frying pan and something to eat with the fish. I'll try to make an effort to control my demands on you!" Amber busied herself with dinner preparations while Cody cleaned the fish and built up the campfire for cooking on.

No meal in the finest restaurant would have made them more content. The beautiful setting, fresh air, crackling fire, and serenade of the squirrel all added to the flavor of the meal they enjoyed creating together. The elk made another appearance, the ducks paddled around in circles, and the fish jumped, making circular ripples in the lake.

"Don't you think ol' Daniel Boone's wildlife theater is better than a stuffy old museum?" Cody took credit for nature's show.

"You sweep a girl off her feet, you do! It is magnificent. There is no place I'd rather be. How can I show my gratitude?" Amber felt like she would burst with happy contentment. They were good together. Her fears were foolish.

They spent the rest of the day in and out of the water as they splashed and laughed at each other. They ran along the lakeshore. They gathered wood for the campfire. They explored paths that led through the trees and back again.

Cody knew each species of trees at a glance. He explained how to identify the ones they saw. Hemlock, with its flaky outer bark that exposed a red-purple layer beneath. The inner wood was darkish, and the branches were spread out with soft flat needles. Pine trees were often pitchy. The bark could be a yellow-green under the dark outer layer. The needles were long on upraised branches. Dark-reddish-barked spruce trees had spikey short needles on their thick branches. Birch had leaves instead of needles, with white bark that peeled like paper. Fir trees had thick dark bark with softer needles, and the inside wood was brownish. Balsam had bark like an elephant's leg and stunk like cat pee if used for firewood. Even the dead dry wood without leaves, needles, or bark was easy for Cody to identify. They would be gathering mainly pine, fir, spruce, and birch for their own wood stove. Amber was soon picking out trees and pieces of logs, trying to identify them. Cody patiently either agreed, or told her why it was a different specie than she thought. Pine and spruce looked the same to her without their needles and branches. Pine had a more orangish wood and spruce bark could show a cup shaped underside if you flaked it off.

Cody's father's occupation was logging long before Cody quit the sawmill to go logging with him. Some of his earliest memories were in his grandfather's pole cutting camp (referred to by his family as the "too short pole camp" due to a measurement mistake) in the middle of a small pine tree forest. His tree knowledge seemed a natural part of his life. Amber's eager interest gave himself respect. His wife seemed proud of him. It was a good feeling he had hungered for. He had gained an eager companion, both to learn from him and help him in any way she could. She helped him realize how much he really knew. She appreciated his smartness.

On their way back to Tesley, Cody stopped to trade his car in on a pickup truck. The salesman wasn't offering them a very good deal and Cody hesitated. The salesman left them alone in "private" to discuss the deal. Amber quoted the price Cody had expected and suggested he stick to it. Surprisingly, as if he'd listened in on their conversation, the salesman came back with that exact offer. Cody made the deal and arranged payments. They drove to their home in the "new to them" truck.

# Chapter 10

The honeymoon was over. It had been a long tiring day. They'd emptied the truck. Amber was busy trying to put some things away and get ready for Cody's work the next day. Cody had finished his relaxing beer.

"Where the hell's the damn alarm clock? I need to set it for work!" Cody demanded.

"I don't know where the 'hell' it is. Why don't you look for it yourself?" Amber retorted.

"You stupid, useless, damn bitch!" Cody yelled at her.

Amber's eyes flashed in fury. She quit what she was doing and found the clock. "Don't ever call me those kind of names! You owe me an apology!" Her voice shook.

"Then don't ever tell me you don't know where the hell something is!" Cody thundered back. "It's your own stupid fault!"

Amber sat down with tears streaming down her face, not knowing pregnancy hormones were adding to her uncontrolled emotions. She trembled and tried to control her sobs. It had been sweetheart, honey, and words of endearment before. Was it over the day they came back from their honeymoon? Could you talk that way to someone you said you loved?

"Oh, for shit's sake! Don't cry now." Cody saw she was really upset for some stupid reason. "I'm sorry, all right? Come on now, let's go to bed and make up, okay?" He went to bed and Amber followed after finishing a few tasks.

Their lives settled into a routine of work, play, and making love. Amber kept busy fixing up their home and visiting friends and family. Wallpapering, painting, and sewing curtains gave a face lift to the house. She thought Cody would look forward to coming home after working all day, but he started to stop for a couple beers with the boys. Amber reheated his dinners for him when he was ready to quit drinking. She tried not to nag and complain, but let him know she wished he'd come home after work. If he responded at all, it would be with a vulgar comment. She tried to get over her hurt and disappointment.

Cody took Amber to see his work site when the crew was gone for the weekend. He wanted to skid a few extra trees down to the landing for the processing crews. He showed her how he pulled the seven cables, called chokers, from the back of the D-6 cat he now operated. He separately wrapped and hooked them around seven logs. A hydraulic lever drew the cables up to the back of the cat, lifting the ends of the logs off the ground. With Amber beside him on the cat, he dragged the logs to the cleared landing where he situated them for the buckermen. They would trim the branches off and buck the logs to desired lengths for the different mills that the logging trucks hauled to. He finished clearing the skid trails, which he explained was where the fallers fell the trees for the cat skidders to drag to the landings for bucking and processing.

These were their best days together. Amber recognized Cody's skill and hard work at his job. He enjoyed the fact that she would want to see what he spent his days doing. She wasn't afraid to climb around and walk with him on the logs even though she was noticeably pregnant. True to his word, Cody took Amber hunting also. She learned not to step on noisy twigs and even walk bowl legged so her jeans wouldn't make rustling noises. Sneezing, coughing, and talking were not allowed unless, of course, Cody had a coughing fit from his heavy smoking. Amber often tapped her puckered lips with her finger, signaling quiet, as he coughed. This would earn her an angry glare or a playful kiss and hug, depending on Cody's mood.

Cody's father Calvin and his buddy Freddy were the longtime hunting partners with him. When his father joked about having the old ball and chain come along, Cody didn't take it as a joke. He quit taking Amber along unless she was the only one available. Whenever

Cody was with his father and other buddies for more than a few drinks, he came back to Amber with a chip on his shoulders. He was ready to verbally abuse her (that's what she labeled it when he belittled her and called her vulgar names). He pushed her roughly if she gave him the slightest reason by defying or disrespecting him in any way. This was a different person from the man she loved. She didn't want to be intimate with that stranger.

"When you're drunk, it's not really you," she tried to explain to him when he was sober. Though she'd always have his dinner ready for him, she'd sometimes pretend to be asleep when he drove home drunk. Most times he would demand dinner to be served by her even if it was still kept warm. It was easier to comply than to fight back. She was reduced to being his convenient possession.

"If you can't come home for dinner, you should be able to get it for yourself!" Amber tried to stand up for herself when Cody complained about his warmed-over dinner being dried out one night. Cody grabbed his plate and threw it, with what was left, onto the ceiling in a blind rage. He tore the clothes off the stupid slut, whore, bitch, useless c———and dragged her to bed. He would have raped her but was too wasted and soon passed out.

Amber crawled out of bed and huddled in the corner of the closet. She drew a blanket around her to muffle her sobs and weeping. What could she do? she wondered. She was expecting a baby so soon with a husband she started to fear more than respect. If only he would be tender and loving again. She fell into a fretful sleep. Suddenly Cody was hovering over her.

"What are you trying to do?" Cody, gruff and hung over, challenged. He was tired of the guilt Amber was always dumping on him, just for having a few drinks or going to a party without her. He even offered to send someone to fetch her once, and she told him she wasn't a dog to be fetched. He brought home a paycheck, didn't he? He worked hard at his job, even if he had to drag himself there with a hangover. He never missed work. Amber begrudged him playing poker with the men and spending his own money. She thought she deserved some spending money also. Hell, he had her name on their bank account to write checks for groceries and to pay bills. Maybe if she kept the house better and was a better cook he wouldn't have got so mad that time she bought something for when the baby was born. She could have sewn something. Maybe he wasn't the same like she said, but she was cramping his style and his fun. Her quiet anger and hurt showed in her eyes. He could get her to do what he wanted all right, but her warmth for him was gone unless he babied her instead of enjoying his freedom to do whatever he wanted. "Grow up, Amber," he said wearily. He reached down to pull her up.

Amber avoided Cody's hand. "*You* grow up and become a responsible person!" She thought fiercely. She scrambled and squeezed past him to their bathroom, locking the door behind her. She bit and pinched herself until the physical pain helped her gain control over her emotional pain. She washed her face in cold water and rubbed the marks she'd made on herself. She took a deep breath, squared her shoulders, and went into the kitchen. Cody had made coffee and was drinking it. She poured herself a cup and politely thanked him for making it. Since he never ate breakfast, she made his lunch for work and another pot of coffee for his thermos. She usually enjoyed getting up early every morning with Cody, even if it was just to have coffee together and make sure he had a freshly made lunch. Sometimes they'd talk a bit, depending on Cody's mood. At least he wanted her with him when he drank his pot of morning coffee.

Staying out of Cody's way, she cleaned up what she could of the plate and food he'd thrown the night before. Cody couldn't remember any of the night but figured he must have made the mess. Amber answered with cool politeness when he asked her what she'd made for his lunch. He put his arm around her when she routinely filled up his coffee. Amber stiffened but otherwise showed no response.

Cody's head hurt. Amber moved away as soon as he released her. The silent treatment was one of the ways Amber tried to make him feel guilty, so must be this cool politeness. She'd get over it. She always did. He knew a hug, a compliment, and a promise to do something together made the love and trust rekindle in her now vacant eyes. She was looking out the window and rubbing a spot on her stomach. He had thrilled at the feel of his child the first time Amber had put his hand on what could have been the baby's foot pushing against him. He put his hand where Amber had been rubbing and felt the movement of the baby. He could feel her trying not to shrink away and saw her jaw was set. He was getting late for work. He'd have to drive fast.

"I love you, honey." He kissed her and hugged her to him. "Give me a hug. It's getting late." Amber's hug was obedient but mechanical. It was going to be a long rough day. He'd have to sweat out his hangover at work. He wondered again what Amber was upset about from last night. He'd maybe let her win this round, by not stopping with the boys for a drink after work.

Suddenly his anger flared at his drinking buddies. There were times when he wished he could just go straight home without the constant razzing about being pussy whipped by the old ball and chain, or questioning if he were a man or a mouse. Many other ways, also, they ridiculed his interest in his own wife and child. Oh ouch, he really didn't feel well. Maybe that would get him out of it better. He'd plead over doing it and needing a day, or even two, to recuperate. He pushed himself through the day's work. They might call him a wimp for going home after, but not for work performance. A man got respect for doing good at his job. His father put lots of importance on work.

*Wonder what he'd have to say if I said Amber was more important to me than anything, the baby too? Being a dependable husband and good father is worth more respect even than work is... He'd say 'She brainwashed you, did she?' and he'd be right. She's brainwashing me. Better stick to the sick excuse.* Cody's thoughts made him curse and sigh.

Amber had spent her day keeping busy. She baked fresh bread and made a nice dinner as an act of faith that things would get better. She fixed herself up as much as she could, feeling so large with child. She had been looking for answers to her marriage muddle. An article in one of those "Gospel Tracts" said women drove their men to drink. It really was all the woman's fault. For its proof, it quoted part of a Bible verse: "It's better to live on a hilltop alone than in a mansion with a contentious woman." She looked up the verse and it had no reference to drinking at all. The article made her so angry and defiant.

*Thank God.* Amber thought. *Al-Anon has a better grip on reality. If it was attitude, I'd be the one drunk. He drank too much before I came along, almost his whole family does. The AA prayer—God, grant me the serenity to accept the things I cannot change, the courage to change the things I cannot accept, and the wisdom to know the difference—is a better basis to keep hope and faith for our marriage alive. Sometimes it's the man who is contentious."* She was going to study more AA literature. *Regardless, I have to choose what kind of wife, mother, and person I want to be. Not through force, domination, manipulation, or a guilt trip, but choice. Neither Cody nor the drunkenness can control who or what I am or could be in happier circumstances. I will keep the vision of a happy home and be who I'd want to be in it.*

Cody half expected Amber to be in a funk, or cool and distant, as he wearily came through their door. It had been a rough day all around. Work had not gone smoothly. He'd been called a wimp for admitting to not feeling well, but at least that was all. He laughed it off, telling them they felt the same way and would be smart to slow down themselves. God knew he needed a drink bad. If he could force down some food and sleep, maybe he could get rid of the empty feeling that plagued him whenever Amber withdrew.

"You're home early," Amber greeted him. "You look tired." She took his lunch kit and thermos and began cleaning them. "Didn't you like your lunch? Sandwiches get dull after a while, don't they?"

"Lunch was fine," Cody said. "I wasn't feeling hungry, but fresh bread and dinner smells good. Would you mind if I have a beer before we eat?" He had needed one all day but found himself asking instead of his normal "Get me a beer!" demand. He began undoing his work boots.

"I'll get you one." Despite her former resolve, Amber's cheerfulness was forced.

Cody's simple "Thank you, sweetheart," however, was a soothing reward to her bruised heart.

She smiled. "Welcome."

"You won't have to undo my boots tonight, Esther." Cody winked as he kicked them off his feet. Arnold's wife Esther, it was well-known, always unlaced his boots for him and helped him take them off. The first time Cody had demanded that Amber unlace his boots, she'd called him Arnold.

"Esther, Esther," she'd playfully mocked in a deep demanding voice, "get your lazy butt over here and undo my boots, Esther!" Then, answering in a higher octave than her own voice replied, "Yes, Arnold, right away, Arnold. What else can I do for you, dear Arnold? I'm so sorry I kept you waiting when you've been working so hard all day and I've just been laying around spending all your hard-earned money." It had become an easy laugh, as well as self-realization. Even Cody's father wouldn't order his mother around like Arnold did Esther.

"I'd better rub your shoulders and back then, Arnold," Amber responded. She gave him a quick massage, paying special attention to the area in his lower backbone that often pained him. "Are you just about ready for dinner?"

Cody tipped up the rest of his beer and nodded. "I needed that beer," he admitted honestly. "Dinner sounds good now. Thanks, sweetheart. You are good to me." He gave her hand a quick squeeze as she went to finish getting their dinner.

*Yesterday a slut, whore, bitch, stupid c——and today a sweetheart… I must have really changed overnight.* Amber pushed the bitter thought away. She had to give each new beginning a chance, didn't she? Fighting Cody didn't fight what controlled him when he turned his anger and frustrations on her. She was no Little Miss Suzy Homemaker by any means…but Cody was usually good natured about that if she catered to him in other ways: Like leaving the dishes for later if he wanted her to go somewhere with him. Like not having a fit if he tracked mud all over her newly mopped floor. He said he liked a house to look lived in, not a showplace you couldn't relax in. She had no knack for organization but was good at making more work for herself by not thinking ahead. Maybe they could both do better together.

Sometimes Cody surprised Amber by his concern when she tripped and almost fell. Other times he was so rough and unfeeling that she felt like screaming, "I'm pregnant! Don't you think you should be a little protective of me?" She didn't though. She was intimidated by his uncontrolled temper, especially when he blared obscenities at her.

The drinking bouts continued. Sometimes Cody was a happy drunk, again promising to make her his queen, that he would be her king, showering her with treasures. Other times he was an angry brute, ready to lash out at her without reason. She had to be very careful not to "poke the bear." When dreams became nightmares, she desperately hung on to her chosen vision of a happy home and family. Though she stumbled and failed lots, she got up to try again.

# Chapter 11

"There's a boat for sale cheap." Cody came home early and excited. "I think we should buy it. We could go up the lake fishing and I could show you all the beaches and islands."

They were keeping up with their payments, Amber's parents had been paid back, and Cody had recently won at poker playing with his buddies. Amber readily agreed, grateful that he seemed to want her approval before going ahead to get whatever he wanted. It would be something they could enjoy doing together also.

Cody soon showed how capable he was at maneuvering the boat and motor for fishing and touring the sights up and down the lake. They made good use of the boat. Amber again admired his quick skill and knowledge. The fresh fish they caught were an added bonus.

The logging company Cody was working for got a contract near Budding and trained him to run their "snipper," a TD bulldozer, with what appeared like giant scissors that he learned to manipulate to fall the trees. He took Amber with him one weekend to finish up the last of the contract. He had become skilled at manipulating the gears and attachments to balance and toss the whole big tree through the air into a pile at the precise moment he completed the "scissors" cut. His neatly made piles would be handy for the skidders to haul to the landings for the buckermen to limb and power saw into sellable lengths. Amber thought it was like riding inside a loud, giant prehistoric dinosaur made of iron as it thrashed through the forest devouring the biggest trees in its path with unbelievable power. She was amazed at his control over the iron beast.

With the contract finished, Cody went back to skidding trees for the company.

When Cody began talking about buying his own machine instead of working with the company's D6 cat, Amber thought it was a good plan. They'd become friends with other young families that had started their own logging business. Cody admired their success. (Amber admired how the husband treasured and showed dedicated respect for his family, but she was wise enough not to point it out.) They searched for and found a D6 cat Cody thought would serve him well. They took out a bank loan in high hopes of success. They made their payments on time, gained equity, but had difficulty paying the taxes on the supposed income gained.

# Chapter 12

Aunty Rose came to visit Amber one day in order to share some of her experience and wisdom about pregnancy and childbirth. "Make sure you get to the hospital in time to have your baby," she warned Amber. "One of my friends used a tomato juice can to pee in during the night. They didn't have indoor plumbing. I got a frantic call from her husband asking me to come help. We had a terrible time getting that baby's head out of that can, let me tell you! Babies can come just that fast. God knows what would have happened if I hadn't come to help."

Aunt Rose had travelled horseback, having to fiord a river, and ride a narrow, unstable mountain path to help a woman whose baby was stuck in the birth canal. Well, she just helped that baby get out in the nick of time before it smothered and the mother would have died also. It had one of those banana heads, though, that babies get if the mother's birth canal is too tight. So she gently massaged and rounded its head up again. After that, it was the cutest baby ever. Fortunately, she'd gotten there in time to help.

Another woman thought she was having a bowel movement and had to retrieve her baby from the toilet. It was sure a good thing they had indoor plumbing instead of having to get it out of the bottom of the outhouse. *Oh yes!* There were so many things that could happen. Like the mother or baby dying in childbirth. Some babies were born with all kinds of deformities or medical problems. It was a good thing Amber didn't do drugs, or the baby would be born addicted.

Aunt Rose was sure Cody would appreciate that she had taken the time out to help Amber get ready and to know what to expect for their baby. If the baby should come before time and be born at home, she would need clean linen and to boil some water. She'd need to have string boiled to tie the baby's umbilical cord that was attached to its belly button or it could bleed to death. Oh, there were so many things that could go wrong. One should be as prepared as they could. It was too bad she had to get back to Uncle Ned, or she could give Amber more of her insight and encouragement.

Amber thanked her for her thoughtfulness in coming to visit. She gave a sigh of relief as she waved goodbye.

When Cody came home, Amber told him that she was glad Aunt Rose had stories so outlandish that it made her laugh instead of being afraid. Many, many women had babies without complications. She'd been born at home okay.

Early one morning (conveniently on a weekend), Amber awoke and found herself in labor. Cody drove her to the hospital in Budding. Amber sat close. "You know I love you and I think you really do want to show love to me, but it's like you're afraid I'd use it against you if you showed it too much." Cody didn't respond but talked about the baby instead. They had over an hour drive to the hospital. Though nervous and excited, they were confident the birth would wait until they were there.

After being admitted, checked, shaved, and waiting for the adequate dilation and bearing down pains to begin, Amber was comforted that Cody was back in the room with her. He, though, was more concerned with his own tiredness than her discomfort. The pain made her nauseous and finally her water broke and the nurses came.

She was wheeled to the delivery room while Cody went for a coffee. Then he went to the waiting room to wait for it to be over so he could see his child. Amber tried to be brave, but when the scrapple was used to slice where she was tearing apart, a squeal squeezed out at the sudden surge in pain. "What is it? Did I have a girl or boy?" she asked.

"Can't tell yet, can't tell by the head. You're not done. Push hard!" the doctor instructed. "You're almost there now."

The miracle of the baby's first cry. The overwhelming love that flooded over Amber as they laid the beautiful baby girl across her. Tears misted her eyes in the wonder of it all. She hardly noticed the stiches given after the placenta flooded out of her. The nurse cleaned them both up and then took the baby to the nursery. She took Amber to her new room.

Cody eagerly identified their baby in the nursery and then went to Amber's bedside. "I heard you scream," he scolded Amber. "I'm glad our baby's okay and everything, but you shouldn't have been so noisy in having her. I was just getting back from getting the coffee I needed, and it scared me. My mom wouldn't have screamed." He showed no extra affection or concern for Amber but hung around to discuss names for the baby. They agreed "Angela" would fit the angelic baby.

The nurse brought Angela in to Amber. Cody held their new baby proudly. He counted her fingers and toes and then rubbed his finger gently across her cheeks. She was rosy colored with dark hair. He had made this baby! He was awesome! He couldn't wait to start celebrating.

Grace, Cody's aunt and Amber's friend, found them in the hospital, having waited there to have her third baby. She was surprised that Angela was born before her own baby and promised they'd get together soon because her contractions were happening strong and hard. Cody charmed the nurses into promising to put Grace into the same room as Amber after her baby was born.

"Got to go home and get ready for work again after I tell everyone about our baby Angela. I'll come and get you and Angela when the hospital says you're ready to go home next weekend," Cody said as he handed the baby back to Amber. He walked away, eager to begin celebrating. He was free from giving Amber another thought until they were ready to come home.

Grace had her baby girl, Sheila, and was wheeled in to share the room Amber was in. Later, when the nurses brought the babies in to be nursed, Grace was getting ready to nurse when Amber looked at the baby that had been brought to her, before putting her to her breast again.

"This isn't my baby! My baby is red faced with dark hair. This baby is yellowish." Amber was ready to panic over her lost baby. The nurses had only brought Angela to Grace, and Sheila, who had a touch of jaundice, to Amber. The mistake was corrected and the babies did have the correct hospital bands that hadn't been checked before. The twin born cousins would grow up to be close friends and teased about "red baby and yellow baby."

When Cody brought Amber and Angela home, he proudly showed Angela to their family and friends. He loved to hold her, making funny noises and faces at her. He swore she knew her dad and smiled at him. Both sets of grandparents and all her aunts and uncles fell immediately in love with Angela.

Angela was a happy, healthy baby thriving on her mother's ample milk. She pulled away from her mother's breast to look at her daddy's face as he made a funny buzzing noise above her with his lips. Amber's milk continued to flow, squirting over Angela's face. The wee girl was shocked into making a funny fish face pout, almost ready to cry. As her parents laughed, she blinked and bravely recovered the business of nursing.

It was exciting to Cody and Amber whenever Angela did something new. Sometimes her cooing sounded like "I love you" to them. Cody had a gift for making Angela laugh and giggle. Amber thought she wanted a dozen precious babies. They had become a family of their own. Cody definitely loved to hold his baby daughter but would gladly hand her over for diaper changes or crying.

# Chapter 13

After boating and fishing half the day, Cody headed for a beach and pulled up the boat safely. He held Angie, while Amber raced behind some bushes to relieve her bursting bladder. Coming back, she saw Cody looking up a path where a tall man was walking toward them. The path led to a well-built house hidden from the view of passing boats.

They exchanged pleasantries. Cody explained that he didn't know anyone lived by this shore where there were no roads. The man said he was a bush pilot who had built a summer hide-away here for his wife and himself. His boat was up the beach a ways.

"Andy Jettings," he introduced himself, extending his hand.

"Cody Bentley, my wife Amber, and little Angela." Cody shook hands.

At the mention of Bentley, Andy blinked. "I know that name… what is your mother and father's name? Do you have any brothers and sisters? What is your mother's maiden name?"

"Calvin and Pamela, Mom used to be a marshal," Cody replied. "Do you know them? I'm the oldest with three brothers and five sisters." Cody pondered how he'd never heard of or met Andy before when he knew almost all his parents' friends, both past and present.

"So you're the baby." Andy looked out across the water. "I met your mother when your grandfather hauled freight and supplies for Tesley. Freight was part of my business too, in supplying camps and mines by airplane. My float plane got grounded in Tesley for a few days." Andy continued. "I got to know your beautiful, fun-loving mother while I waited to repair my plane with the parts your grandfather was bringing back for me. To make a long story short, the next time I had a chance to fly into Tesley, I learned she had married Calvin Bentley and was already expecting their first child." Andy bent over Angela and softly tickled her cheeks as she smiled at him.

"May I hold her, son?" Andy asked Cody. "Hi, little princess. You're beautiful." He gently and tenderly took Angie from her father's arms. Cody and Amber were proud of how she cooed and smiled back at the stranger who so obviously loved babies.

"She often makes strange," Amber said. "You must have a magic touch. You're just like Cody is with babies."

"The way she's growing," Cody teased, "we should try to start another one soon." He loved to see Amber blush. She was grateful Andy's attention was on little Angie.

"Andy," a voice near the house called, "Andy, lunch is ready."

Reluctantly Andy handed Angie back to Amber and shook Cody's hand again as his other hand lingered on Amber's arm. "God bless you all," he said, his eyes moist. Blinking, he grinned and laughed. "I'd better go before I'm lunch…Thank you!" He nodded and then headed for his home. "Coming, love," he called as he quickly went up the path without looking back.

"Wonder if your mom will remember him since he's almost as sexy as you are," Amber joked. "Strange how you can meet someone in the middle of nowhere and feel like you know them. You even look like him and are the same with babies. He sure loved Angela, didn't he? Of course, what's not to love!"

"Yeah," Cody agreed. "Can you imagine flying a plane and seeing all these lakes and mountains from the sky? Let's see if this old motor will start." They headed back down the lake toward home.

Thrilled with their daughter, they spent time together as a family. The happy grandparents babysat for short times, allowing just them to go hunting or do other things together. Drinking bouts still caused problems, but for the most part, their passion for each other and their baby won out. Spending less time partying and poker playing, also left more money for Cody's "toys." He loved having his own boat and wanted a better one. Upgrading their house was less important.

Cody forbade Amber to ride her motor scooter before and after Angela was born, but allowed Freddy to try it out. When Freddy brought it back wrecked, he felt justified in telling Amber that it was good she couldn't use the killing machine anymore. Amber felt hurt and resentful of the restraints Cody dominated her with.

# Chapter 14

Amber had attempted over the years to get her birth registered. Finally she obtained forms to fill out and have notarized. Her aunt, who had stayed with them in her first days of life, signed an affidavit. Her parents signed another one. Her baptismal certificate, immigration certificate, and her marriage license, along with all the other forms and records of her schooling, provided just enough proof to finally register her birth. She could finally purchase a birth certificate! She couldn't help but order two, just to be sure in case she lost one. Her baptism certificate had gotten her an American SIN card, so she could work during high school years, but it had been tricky without the birth certificate. Now, at last, she had a birth certificate to show to Canadian authorities. She could get anything that required proof of her birth! She had written proof with a government seal that she was a real person who belonged in this world! She showed it to Cody with excited pride.

"You should go for your Canadian citizenship now," he dryly suggested. "Then you wouldn't be just another stupid damned Yankee." Amber took his razzing with a grain of salt and applied for her Canadian citizenship.

"I'll bring home the bacon, honey," Cody had instructed. "You cook it…and quit burning it." Amber was a stay-at-home mom, glad she still had the freedom of her own car. She cooked, baked, gardened, raised chickens, and picked wild berries. She canned up vegetables from the garden and meat from fishing and hunting. She took her car into Budding to stock up on groceries with his aunt Grace, who had become a best friend to her. She painted, did minor repairs, wallpapered, and sewed and mended clothes.

Amber was almost due with their second child when she went huckleberry picking with Grace and their daughters. Such a good crop meant lots of pies and preserves to please Cody with. Later that night, she went into early labor. Perhaps bending over her big belly caused her to go into the labor pains.

Cody brought her into Budding, but her labor stopped, much to Amber's disappointment. They returned home with Cody resenting how much extra trouble Amber caused him. At her due date, Cody sent her in to stay with friends in Budding, just in case she went into labor while he was at work. His sister, Alice, would look after him and Angie while Amber was gone. Amber went into labor for real. Their friends brought her to the hospital. Amber tried to contact Cody. His sister answered the phone…so she left the message with Alice.

Cody was in the bar. His sister found him there drunk. He was putting an empty beer bottle up a woman's skirt, just as a joke, of course. Cody figured the doctors and nurses were all Amber needed and kept drinking. Aahhh, still some real freedom to be and do what he loved! He was the real man's man.

The next morning Cody recognized the two long and three short rings of their telephone. He put down his coffee and dragged himself over to answer. "Get off the line, Aunt Rose," he said before Amber could say anything more than a weak "Cody?" She told him he had a son. It wouldn't be necessary to tell anyone else in town the news. Rose hadn't got off the line.

Cody managed a quick trip into Budding to see his son. A son and a daughter, he was so proud of his accomplishment. His boy was born with long dark hair already. They decided to call him Carey. Carey's cry was loud and strong. He was hungry. Amber put him to her breast while Cody watched. His boy was born knowing how to drink his fill. The nurse came in to massage the grapefruit-sized clot forming inside Amber from a complication with the afterbirth. Cody held his son and managed to burp him. It was good to have seen his wonderful son. He'd come back when they were ready to come home. Now he had people to tell and celebrate with. He handed Carey back to Amber.

"Keep massaging this off and on," the nurse continued to show Amber. "If it doesn't dissolve, they may have to operate. Nursing your baby might help also." The nurse was interested in how Amber was doing as well as how the baby was. Cody strode away to enjoy his freedom to celebrate.

To Amber's relief, the hard ball dissolved. Carey was greedy for his mother's milk and so awesome. What beautiful, perfect babies they'd had. They made life good, and Amber said a prayer of thanks to God.

"There's a hockey game on, and it's a damned good one!" Cody grumbled. "Just stay in town with the Mortens for a while. Call them to pick you up if you can't walk there. I'll come and get you after the game." He hung up on Amber's protests that he should be responsible to pick them up, not the Mortens. He finished his beer and reached for another. It was time to go to his dad's house again to watch the hockey game with the gang. He loved the hockey games and the play offs. Maybe his son would grow up to be a hockey player. He could imagine the admiration he'd get then. A son!...Oh what the f——ing hell. Maybe he'd go get his son and find out about the game after, like his nagging, fishwife insisted.

Meanwhile the nurses scolded Amber for crying. They told her it would affect her milk for the baby if she let herself get upset. She needed to hold it together for her children. She got up and washed her face and hands to get ready to nurse Carey. She cradled him in her arms with overwhelming love. Such an alert, eager baby. She finished nursing and burping him. He was being fussier than usual. Maybe it was her milk? She dressed them both and made sure they were ready to leave the hospital before she had to make the dreaded call to the Mortens. She cuddled and kissed Carey, stroked his long dark baby hair, praying for courage. As she laid him back down to phone, there was Carey heading for their son.

"I'm so glad you came!" her voice squeaked with emotion.

"You owe me big time now!" he replied angrily. "Get the rest of your junk. Let's go. Maybe we can get back in time to see part of the game." He carried Carey as Amber obediently followed.

With deep sadness, Amber thought, *Am I not also owed anything? Is everything always about you? What you want? Don't I count for even a tiny little bit? You're always the center of your own universe where I'm only there to serve you. You might think you're such a man's man, but you bully me like a spoiled, selfish child.*

# Chapter 15

Amber started to dread answering the phone. She felt like hiding from the outside world. She was tired, listless, and bewildered. Carey was a colicky baby and needed a lot of attention. She did what she had to, to take care of her family's needs. She started bottle feeding Carey when she quit producing enough milk for him. Two-year-old Angela was already potty-trained and talking well. As much comfort as her children gave her, however, her marriage depressed her.

Cody was rough with Amber, both physically and verbally. Maybe she was the loser he said she was, and lucky he still put up with her. More than once, she slipped out of bed when he passed out after taking her. She huddled under a blanket in their closet, struggling not to let the children in the adjoining bedroom hear her sobs. Other times her body would respond as she craved the love that seemed missing. Why deny herself pleasure? At least he still desired her and was probably not sleeping around if he wanted her so often. She wished he would brush his teeth and shower more often but would never dare to say it. She subconsciously dressed in less appealing ways in a hidden hope to be left alone.

Amber saw that some marriages were actually a partnership where both enjoyed doing what they could for each other. Cody didn't seem to appreciate anything she did for him but never thought it was enough. If she asked for anything at all, he bellowed a stream of obscene language and accused her of nagging him. Was she supposed to be some kind of robot that obeyed his every command? He showed more respect for his television shows than he did for her.

The children were used to Cody not trusting Amber near other men and felt they should keep an eye on their mother for him. She had started to take them to Sunday school and church. They couldn't wait to tell Cody how mom had held the hymnbook with a man in church and even talked with men and women there.

"You have to watch her even in church," Cody assured them. "She's a stupid slut, always looking for someone to think she's something special or something. Damn bitch."

"I can't believe you'd read anything into sharing a hymnbook when there wasn't enough to go around. You should trust me by now. I've never given you any reason not to. Yet you can call me down in front of the children." Amber shook her head sadly. "I realize you don't think I'm anything worthwhile or you'd treat me like I mattered to you." She put the lunch on the table without further comment.

Cody finished his lunch and then grabbed his beer and whiskey and walked out the door. Amber, Angela, and Corey had gone to church, so he was going out to do his thing, but he didn't have to tell them where. No one seemed to be in a party mood or ready to play poker, so he ended up at his parents for a few drinks. Finally, Freddy showed up and they went out in Cody's boat for a few hours. They both got stinking drunk before heading back, nearly out of booze. Freddy tripped into Cody as he was trying to park his boat. Next thing they knew, they were spun around as the throttle went forward and the boat motor crashed into hidden boulders. Freddy's body took out the windshield. He laughed at Cody's concern for his boat, telling Cody it looked toothless without the windshield. Cody tied up the boat, deciding to check it out some other day. They stumbled to his truck. With practiced drunken skill, Cody drove Freddy home and then went home too.

After Cody was served dinner and Amber had put the children to bed, he told her that the boat might be wrecked by Freddy.

"What were you two doing, going out in the boat when you were both drunk?" Amber was incredulous.

When the plaster wall cracked behind her head as Cody threw her against it, Amber felt helpless. She knew she'd have to leave with the children and get out on her own. Cody had often threatened to find someone else who would let him do whatever he wanted. Well, now he could try. He'd continually told her that no one else would want her, but she wondered how many women would want to be treated like she had been treated.

# Chapter 16

Amber knew nothing of welfare or of women's shelters. Her sister let her move in with her family. The job that Amber got as a waitress was not enough to support herself and her children. She knew she was taking unfair advantage of her sister. Did she have any other alternatives?

Cody wrote her a loving letter asking her to come back. He felt like he was dying. His nerves were shot. His hands shook so bad that he could hardly work. He needed his family. He needed her to come back. *So…she went back.*

Amber's mind blacked out a lot of that dark time of adjustment. Cody controlled himself not to use physical abuse, but his hurt pride continued to spill out verbal abuse. Heavy drinking often continued. Amber became pregnant again. She thought she would lose her mind. It was all so hopeless. "God, please help us," she prayed desperately.

"I had to sell your beer bottles to get milk for the children. You spend all your paychecks on booze and gambling," Amber railed at Cody. "You don't care about anything or anyone but yourself and your whore of drinking!"

"I'm just a f——ing loser," Cody reacted. "I'm no f——ing good. Maybe if I f——ing kill myself, you and the kids would be happy! *You want to leave me again, you f——ing bitch.* I'll show you this time!" Cody grabbed his hunting gun and looked for bullets. He was cursing, yelling, and swearing as he put the bullet in the gun.

Amber and the children were terrified. "Daddy, don't hurt Mommy," blended with Amber's pleas.

"Don't act like this in front of the children. Cody, please, please, I beg you, please."

Cody ran out into the night and fired his gun. It seemed like an eternity before he stood next to the children's bedroom door. "Don't f——ing mess with me, you f——ing slut, c——bitch, or next time it will happen." He stumbled off to bed.

Amber tried to comfort and calm their children. "Daddy's going to sleep now. When he wakes up, everything will be better. It's okay now. Don't worry, I'll stay with you. We have to be careful though. Try to be extra good when Daddy's home." The children quit crying and settled down as she gently tucked them into bed. She patted them and stroked their heads as she tried to sing quietly. "Sleep, my child, and peace attend thee, all through the night. Guardian angels, God will send thee, all through the night." Her off-key voice quavered in unshed tears. The children escaped her singing into peaceful sleep.

A quote popped into Amber's mind: "It's always darkest before the dawn." She stayed with her children, thankful they could sleep. Would the darkness ever recede?

A month later, the twins were born, but one didn't make it. Cody made sure Amber knew she was responsible for any and every bad thing that could ever happen to their children. She was lucky that cute little Cybil was healthy and normal. She better made sure she took really good care of them. It would be her fault if anything ever happened. Amber had been strict with the children trying to make them aware of acceptable and unacceptable behavior but became even stricter. Maybe she subconsciously tried even harder to demand better standards with Carey.

# Chapter 17

Amber became secretly involved in Al-Anon. Her precious Cybil thrived on Amber's breast milk as their other children had. She was so cute and plump, and her older sister loved her. Carey thought she was a cute, nice baby, but Mom should go back and get a boy also. Cybil loved attention, smiling and cooing as soon as she got noticed, even if she had to make a fuss first to get the attention.

Once Cybil was weaned, Amber got her tubes tied without Cody trying to stop her decision. Being a wife and mother where there was constant tension, shattered her expectations of having a large happy family. She realized also that her thinking had become unstable if Cody was to be kept happy as possible at all times, at all costs.

"Make the kids quit bothering me," Cody would say when tired. Other times they would squeal with delight as he hoisted them up to reach the ceiling. They were in awe of his stories. They believed their daddy was truly the strongest dad there ever was, just like he said. He would get them to flex their muscles in their arms to see if they could get them to pop up like his did. They loved his attention.

"What was it like when you were little, Dad?" the children asked Cody.

"My brothers and sisters and I did a lot of hiking and fishing, but we had to be home by dark. We could do almost anything we wanted as long as we were outside. We stole a loaf of raisin bread out of someone's car one day when we were starving after fishing and hiking all day. Once we were playing robbers and cowboys. Your uncle was a cattle wrestler so we were going to hang him. We made a good noose, and he got up on a box and put his head in, but our grandma came out and stopped us before we could kick the box out from under him. So he lived!"

"Went to school with Dolly Parton. Sat right behind her. Got into big trouble for dipping her pigtail in my inkwell. We had inkwells in our desks back then to fill our pens with," Cody convinced them it was a true story. They told all their friends and believed it for years.

"Look out! Get down, watch out!" Cody sprang off the couch where he was sleeping to push Angela out of the way of an unseen danger. Angela willingly flattened herself into the rug to escape whatever it was. When Cody woke up with a puzzled look on his face, they all had to laugh.

"Daddy's home," Amber called out. The children always came to greet him excitedly. Daddy would tickle, tease, and get them to bring his beer and untie his boots while they eagerly told him whatever was on their minds.

He could awe the children and make them laugh. He was so much fun when he wanted to be. If their limited furniture broke with the rough housing, that was Amber's problem…she wasn't much for being a good housekeeper anyhow. The stick in the mud always wanted them to go outside to wrestle around. "Mom's no fun," he reassured them. "Don't listen to that old crab."

*It's true*, Amber thought. *I've forgotten how to have fun. I'm tired and worried all the time.* She remembered the time she had found the children with the bottle of dish soap squirted on the hallway floor. They were running and sliding through it, just having a great time, squealing with delight. She'd recognized the fun they were having and laughed for a moment. Then she remembered that another bottle would have to be bought. She couldn't let them think it was all right to waste and make a mess that she'd have to clean up. What if they were to hurt themselves? Mom wouldn't let Dad be too mean to them, but she could be mean too. Yes, Mom was there if they were scared, hurt, sad, hungry, or needed something…but Dad was fun, though scary!

Cody had slowed down on drinking away from home. His "buddies" had embarrassed him, by painting his face when he drank himself to sleep in the bar. Some of the old gang had settled down with families of their own, making the bar less fun also. He no longer used the excuse of a messed up house and the nagging wife to stay out. It was cheaper to drink at home, but not as easy to drink as much with Amber and the children distracting him.

Amber stared out the window, immobilized. She had been helpless to create a well-groomed home for her husband and children. She was not accomplishing anything anyhow. Why not go outside with her children? They could play in the snow together for around an hour a day. She was surprised by the extra energy and ability to concentrate on her other tasks that taking the time outside gave her. She even found a way to hook up swings into their attic roof so the children could wear off some of their extra energy when they came back inside. She fixed up the two upstairs rooms so Angela and Cybil could share one, and Carey could have the one with the swings in it. She told them to make sure they went down the outside balcony stairs if there was ever a fire. The extra room made things seem less cluttered.

"Mom, Mom," the children were screaming during the night. "I think there is a bat flying around." They continued screaming, terrified of the stories they'd heard of bats flying into the hair and giving them rabies. Amber raced up the stairs, and sure enough, it was a bat hanging on the wall above Angie's bed.

Amber raced back down stairs and quickly came back with a gallon jar that she slipped the bat into and closed the lid on it. After getting a close-up look at the captured bat, the children were more fascinated than afraid. If Mom would bring the jar with the bat downstairs, they wanted to look at it some more in the morning. "Wait till Dad sees what was in our room!" They looked forward to sharing their news. Amber read them another bedtime story (as was her normal routine) to settle them down again before going back to bed herself.

# Chapter 18

It was late at night on the holiday weekend. Tesley had an influx of out of towners, with teams heading to play baseball, or heading for fishing, boating, or just enjoying camping by the beaches. Amber and the children were sound asleep. She woke up to the sound of someone racing a truck motor in their yard.

*Maybe Cody's back from playing poker or partying or wherever he's been,* she thought as she peaked out the window. It wasn't him by the looks of it. An old truck, with a driver she didn't recognize, was now idling in their yard. She could tell the driver wasn't the only one in the truck. She became afraid for her children's safety.

She remembered the BB gun she still had from her parents' farm. She quietly pulled it out from the top of the closet. After practicing to see if she could get her voice, she threw the door open, making sure the gun was visible in front of her. Trying to sound threatening, she said loudly, "You better get out of here and go somewhere else to park."

"Whoa," the driver said, "Cody said he lives here. I was just bringing him home 'cause he's in no shape to drive." He turned to Cody. "Can you make it out all right?"

"Told you my wife was a stupid, idiot bitch," Cody told his driver as he stumbled out of the truck toward where Amber stood with her empty gun. "She's one son of a bitch f——ing nutcase!"

"Looks to me like she's pretty darn brave," the driver stated. He backed around and left.

Amber helped Cody the rest of the way inside to the couch before getting him the beer he demanded. He passed out with some of the beer spilling over. Amber cleaned it up, tossed a blanket on him, and went back to bed.

A neighbor offered Amber part-time work. Another agreed to babysit. Cody surprised her by agreeing. The work was cleaning a bunk house that she could walk to.

"Guess I'll give up bringing home all the bacon idea since it's only a few hours a week…you burn the bacon anyhow." He smiled.

Soon Amber was working four hours a day as the crew's morning cook also. Maybe it was easier to clean and cook where one didn't have to go back and do it again the same day. Amber asked to buy a second hand clothes dryer with one of her paychecks. Cody reluctantly agreed. Amber made Cody feel like a hero for agreeing. Maybe he wasn't giving her too much freedom after all. Her earnings were subject to him still. Maybe she knew better than to think anything was really hers.

The little spin washer that Gert and Rob had given them (Amber often had to go to a spring down the road and pack water when their well went dry or water line froze) could keep up with the clothes and cloth diapers. To conserve water and soap, Amber would sort clothes in small loads from the cleanest whites to the dirtiest darks. Wash and spin each load and then change the water. The same system was used to rinse each load, unless the rinse water looked dirty enough to need a second rinse. The clothes were hung outside to hopefully dry. Often the clothes froze and had to be brought back in to finish drying. Sometimes she brought them in to avoid a rainstorm rewetting them when they were almost dry. With the dryer to use, the house wouldn't be cluttered with almost dry clothes! She promised to only use the dryer for clothes she couldn't dry on the clothesline.

Cody and Amber both wanted rainy-day money in the bank. His pickup trucks, their home, and his logging equipment were the only things to go into debt for. Cody made a good living, but an extra income helped when they wanted to buy things for cash, like a new freezer.

When Cody came across a good deal on a small used snow mobile, he bought it for ice fishing. Their children enthusiastically spent hours riding it around and pulling each other (sometimes dangerously) on a sled while Cody was at work. Later he generously bought a small motorcycle that they so enjoyed. Amber may have looked like a big kid, but she rode it also. Cody let them have a dog that was offered to them. He loved and enjoyed his children and gave them what he could. His own wants, however, always came first.

In spite of the dysfunctional family life they started in, their children were growing up normal and healthy. The girls had to be reassured, by Amber at times, that they were slender, beautiful, good girls and not fat sluts with huge butts. They all possessed a good sense of humor and responsibility. They were getting into some but not too serious trouble. The tree fort they burnt down with a poorly placed candle didn't catch the woods on fire but gave them more respect for the danger of fires.

Cody hired a handyman to put a good water system into their house and enjoyed the improvement himself. Too many times he was hearing, "My wife would never put up with…" He wanted respect from his peers. After Amber made good money by planting trees, Cody agreed when Amber wanted to take a log scaling course to find a better paying job and looked forward to the extra income he'd have access to. When they were hunting and getting their winter's wood together, he even reinstructed her on all the species of trees she would need to be able to identify.

# Chapter 19

Amber often tried to ridicule Cody for his drinking when she felt like defending herself in a safe group setting. She resented and held grudges for past hurts. She wasn't willing to sink into the past helpless despair and was trying to let it go to quit fearing the future.

"I am no good for you or myself," Amber told sober Cody as she held him close, "when I tear you apart because of what the drinking does to us. I'll never be free from loving you. You'll always be a part of me. I'll only ever leave you if I have to go to keep the drinking from destroying us both. Please don't make me go."

Secretly, Amber continued to communicate with Al-Anon friends. She understood that the drinking could only control her life if she allowed it to. She found that she could enjoy the good times more if she wasn't dragging the bad times into them. She promised herself to treat her husband as if he were the man he could be, the one she loved and respected. That was the kind of wife she wanted to be. She broke and repeated the promise often. She found laughter was their best medicine.

Clumsily Amber knocked over a jar of change Cody had been saving, and he roared at her angrily. "I'm not afraid of you anymore!" she challenged. Then she laughed as she scurried to pick up all the coins and replace the jar to a safer place. She purposely bumped playfully into Cody, and he had to laugh and hug her.

"Mom's going to babysit. We're going to the Green Rock Hall to a dance party," Cody announced. "I'll take the kids up there now. You get ready. Wear that little blue dress you made. It looks good on you."

"Thank you!" Amber lit up at the unexpected compliment and prospect of a date night.

Cody started drinking whiskey as he drove out. "You can't bring your booze inside," he explained. Half an hour later, when they arrived, the dance was in full swing. They went right inside. After a couple dances with Amber, Cody went outside for a couple drinks with the guys. Amber was quickly whisked back out onto the dance floor. She was enjoying the rhythmic music and friendly partners. Suddenly Cody was pulling her outside and pushing her into his truck.

"Can't leave you alone for a minute, you filthy, dirty, f——ing, slut, whore, and you forget you have a husband. You dumb whore," Cody slurred in a drunken jealous rage.

"You left me at the dance and I was just dancing," Amber retorted in a huff.

Then Cody was choking her and everything was going black. Instinctively Amber went limp instead of fighting him. Cody began shaking her, insisting she was a stupid bitch and a fake. When he was satisfied that she was actually breathing and okay, he was ready to go back into the dance. "Come on!" he roughly pulled at her.

"*No!* You just tried to kill me, Cody!" Amber hissed. "I'm not going anywhere!" Angry tears stung her eyes. Cody was capable of murderous rage.

"What the f——ing hell, you stick in the mud baby." Cody lurched back into the truck and roared the motor to life. He had plenty of practice driving drunk and made it safely home. Amber had huddled away from Cody and toyed with the idea of opening the door and rolling out of the moving truck, but thoughts of their children kept her from going through with it. She jumped out as soon as he stopped the truck. She turned the motor off, grabbing the keys on the way. Cody passed out in the truck.

*He can freeze to death for all I care,* Amber thought angrily. The thought of "God hears your murderous thoughts" shook her. She went back out with a warm sleeping bag to cover him. "At least I can sleep alone to escape my thoughts."

When Cody woke up, he went inside. Amber was in the children's old room instead of theirs. He left her alone and crawled into their bed. Amber was drinking coffee when he woke up again. "I'm really sorry about last night," he surprised Amber, both that he remembered and that he apologized. Still, she wasn't about to say it was all right. "I'll go get the kids after I have coffee. Do you want to go with?"

She'd wait at home. She needed to find some strength in the Al-Anon literature and in prayer. She'd see if he meant his apology before making any plans about their future.

As the children grew, they were protective of their mom. Little Cybil stood with her hands on her hips and her eyes flashing fire after she watched Carey and Angela push Mommy out of the way of the vacuum hose as Daddy swung it at Mommy and broke the window. (Amber had made the mistake of saying the vacuum Cody had made the sacrifice of buying her was a lemon without suction.) "You better not be mean to my mommy!" she threatened as she stamped her foot in defiance.

The children were almost all in their teens soon. Cody would take his family ice fishing or boating, fishing, and camping. He and Carey had bonded over hunting and fishing. He was still drinking but trying to be more of a family man. He was more gentle with Amber. When he lost his temper, swearing and calling her names, she just told him he didn't mean it. That he really meant: sweetheart, darling, love of my life, my beautiful, kind, loving, exciting wife, so smart, and sexy too. He started calling her lover bug, and she called him lover man. The children were embarrassed but delighted. They all laughed with the new exchanges.

# Chapter 20

Cody worked hard and dressed for the minus-forty-degree cold snap. Extremely frozen equipment needed to be kept running or started every couple of hours to warm up in order to work. Cody had bought an old parachute to cover the D6 bulldozer cat that he and the bank now owned. He had a propane blow torch in order to heat the oil and hydraulics to get his machine to start. Skid trails needed to be pushed in for the fallers. Just an ordinary day, working with the elements. His bulldozer was an older one with a protective grate, but no solid enclosure to protect him from the weather. The large radiator fan, turned backward for the cold, blew some heat in. The fallers had gone and the buckermen were on their way home and Cody was looking forward to finishing up the skid trails that were needed. Suddenly a severely frozen willow caught and broke in the grate. As it snapped, a piece shot like a bullet into Cody's eye.

Bleeding, weak, and in shock, he threw his machine out of gear and stumbled to the landing holding the side of his face, hoping to find help. The first aide attendant was just leaving. Thankfully the first aide attendant saw him and rushed him to the nearest hospital in Budding over two hours away. The doctor immediately determined he would have to be flown to a larger hospital in Vancouver. They were not equipped to deal with the serious injury to his eye in Budding.

As soon as she was notified, Amber made arrangements with family and friends for their children and rushed to Cody's side. Cody had remained conscious through it all. "How bad is it?" she asked the doctor.

"Worst case scenario, he could lose sight in both eyes. Best case scenario, he might be able to see the same as always in one eye and shadows in the injured one. Even though one eye appears uninjured, it could develop what is called 'sympathy' damage by his brain's reaction. They will know more after he's transferred to Vancouver and begins to heal." The doctor gave them a straightforward answer.

Though Amber wanted to stay by his side, Cody was soon flown out. She raced back to Tesley. She promised her children that their dad would be okay. She arranged for them to be looked after if she stayed in Vancouver for a while. Family and friends came to their aide immediately. Amber was able to pack a suitcase and get ready to make the long drive early the next morning to join Cody. City traffic terrified her, but she found her way there.

The big hospital was overwhelming to Amber, but a friendly receptionist assisted her in finding her way to Cody's bedside. Cody had gone through several tests and examinations. Happy to have her with him, Cody filled Amber in on whatever he could. He was settled into a room with a young hockey player whose eye had gotten injured during his game. Cody's aunts and uncles, who lived in Vancouver, had already been to visit him. Amber, they had generously offered, would be staying with them. One uncle would pick her up at the other aunt and uncle's home on his way to work, and the other would bring her back at the end of his work day. She wouldn't have to deal with finding her way and could leave Cody's truck where she'd be staying. She and Cody could have the days together. The hospital had a decent cafeteria where she could buy her meals. It was all planned out.

A couple days later, Cody's doctor came by his bedside with several interns. "This," he explained to his crew and Cody and Amber, "is what is called a black ball. You can see the eye is entirely black and dead without any chance of sight left. He'll be getting a prosthetic eye after he recovers from its extraction and the insertion of the back shield that will be attached to the necessary nerves and muscles. Eye transplants are the imagination of science fiction." They carried on to the hockey player who was expected to have full recovery of sight without complications.

Cody was courageous and took no offence to being on display. He joked with the doctors and nurses with his unique ability to feel at home in any circumstance. "There are so many Wings and Wongs in Vancouver telephone books," he quipped to his perky Chinese nurse, "I might wing the wong one." He interacted easily with those around him with good-natured courage. The comfort of having Amber there to laugh at his jokes and stay beside him made his ordeal bearable.

Soon he was craving his cigarettes and determined to make it to the smoke room down the hall. Ever obliging, Amber spotted an odd-looking wheelchair in the hallway not being used. She figured it should be safer for her to wheel him down the hall in it. So, with his med drip pole between his legs and Amber pushing behind, they made it to the smoke room and back. Questioned by the nurse on their return, Cody admitted to really needing a smoke.

"Did you know that chair is a commode?" she asked with a chuckle.

Cody asked what a commode was as Amber's realization made her giggle. "It's for going to the toilet in when you can't make it to the bathroom. Are we ever a couple of country hicks?"

The nurse made a regular wheelchair available to the rednecks. She still had to grin every time they used it.

"I was born in this hospital," Cody reminisced. "We moved back and forth from Tesley to a border town when there wasn't enough work for Dad, so he took work down here once in a while. Grace and I used to walk across the border to see movies and go roller skating in Mason. It used to be a lot easier to get across, just had to say where you were going and what you were planning to do."

"My sister and I used to roller skate quite a bit. Did you know how to skate very well?" Something was stirring Amber's memory.

"No, Grace could skate better than me. I fell a lot," Cody admitted.

"Was that you?" Amber exclaimed. "A boy who was all arms and legs trying to skate around the rink? He came and talked to me when I was tying my skate back up. He said he could ice skate. He pointed out his aunt to me."

"It had to be. I lied about being able to ice skate, just wanted an excuse for not being able to roller skate. We moved back to Tesley to stay just after that. Then I did learn to ice skate."

"My sister was a little sarcastic when I told her about the boy that had talked to me. She asked me if I was going to marry him or something. It's totally unbelievable that I did!"

Cody laughed. "Do you realize how many years we didn't even know we'd met before? It's crazy, who'd have guessed? It must have been destiny. We were meant to be together!"

The operation to finish removing Cody's eyeball was scheduled. It also meant attaching the back shield to nerves and muscles that would allow his prosthetic eye to move along naturally with his good eye. He could expect initial pain as the nerves and muscles adjusted to the shield. Once successfully done and healed, he would be fitted for the prosthetic eye.

Before the operation, Cody was to bathe. There was a private bathroom where Amber accompanied Cody to scrub his back and help him in and out of the tub. Cody was feeling frisky. "I'm so horny," he entreated Amber. They both knew they would wait until he was out of the hospital.

Cody told Amber that after waking up from the operation, he was screaming and cursing in pain, swearing at everyone who could hear to give him something for the pain. "I sure wasn't horny anymore," he added grimly.

As soon as his nerves and muscles adjusted enough that he could tolerate the shield, Cody quickly weaned himself from pain killers, not wanting to get addicted. He was ready for the prosthetic eye. He would no longer have to look like a pirate with a black eye patch on his face to cover the empty eye socket.

Amber went with Cody for his appointment to be fitted for the prosthetic eye. They learned how the colors were meticulously painted so close to the real eye that it would pick up the same light reflections that made eyes appear different colors by the color and light around them. The muscles attached to the backdrop would move the glass eye in natural likeness of the real eye. It was possible to rub it out of position to weirdly point in another direction though.

The artist picked up a glass eye from his display of eyes. "Heavy drinker," he chuckled as they looked at the red, bloodshot veins painted in the white of the eye. As he completed the steps to fit and insert the new prosthetic, he explained, "You'll need to come back in about a year, because your eye socket will become more sunken. I'll need to make another larger prosthetic that will again fit better and look more natural. You'll know for sure it's time to come back if your glass eye falls out suddenly, like when you rub it." He showed Cody how to pop it out and get it back in to clean it or get it back pointed in the right direction. The prosthetic would have a red dot that would be hidden by the bottom of his eyelid.

Cody returned home wearing his prosthetic eye. They happily reunited with their children and resumed family life together. It had been a traumatic experience for the children to be without their parents even though they were well cared for and hadn't caused their caretakers much trouble. Some of their schoolwork suffered from the stress, though.

Amber took care of the countless forms and phone calls regarding the accident. WCB (Worker's Compensation Board) gave Cody an ultimatum, deciding he should be able to return to work. He was no longer entitled to the compensation wage he'd received in the hospital. They could give him a complete buyout where all future expenses would be his responsibility, or he could choose a small monthly check for the remainder of his life and they would cover the expense of his prosthetic upkeep, including travel costs for it. No thought whatever was given by those powers that trauma also accompanied his accident and there would be no work available for him in his usual type of work during springtime when the bush was too wet and fragile to allow logging.

"Logging industry shuts down this time of year when the bush is too easily damaged by logging. He is not ready to go back to work where there are no jobs in his line of work to go back to! He is in a severely traumatized state. He's not able to collect the unemployment he faithfully paid into for years, because he was self-employed when the accident happened. How can he retrain or find work? You can't just drop him now and expect him to survive further trauma! You're throwing him to the wolves!" Amber angrily argued. She wrote letters and made phone calls to WCB. She asked Cody's doctors to intervene and explain that trauma should be covered by WCB also. Her pleas fell on deaf ears. Cody accepted the monthly pittance. If he lived for more than another ten years, it would add up to the buyout and the claim would remain in effect for upkeep expenses. There was nowhere else to turn.

# Chapter 21

Cody turned back to drink. How could a logger with one eye get work where there was no work to be had? Tesley's highway foreman was aware of their situation. A small gravel spreading contract was offered Cody. Amber felt her prayers had been answered. They wouldn't lose Cody's equipment. When the job was done, he needed to look for work again. Welfare was not an option for them. They sold a trailer they had acquired. Bills were piling up.

Cody used his sense of humor for those who asked about his glass eye. He went hunting with his friends and shot moose and deer. "I don't have to close one eye to focus anymore," he joked. He pretended to pop the eye out and hold it under the table where several ladies in party dresses sat. "I can see what color your underwear is!" He saved the first prosthetic that had been replaced and allowed curious young children to examine it. He did have to quit baseball because his depth perception was off. His days of hitting the ball out of the park were over. He was still able to adjust enough to skillfully operate equipment and drive.

Through friends and a chain of events, Cody's logging equipment was hired near a northern town by the Alaska border. There was no work in Tesley. Their cluttered house was cleared out, storing whatever they could in a shed. They found renters for their house who would move in when they left.

Cody, Amber, and their teenagers Carey and Cybil packed up and moved farther north. Angela moved in with her aunt and uncle to finish school and train for being a dental assistant.

Carey and Cybil were enrolled in their new school and almost immediately fitted in and made good friends. They found good summer jobs also. Cybil was voted Miss Congeniality for the May Day Queen contest.

But nothing was easy for any of them. Outrageously high rent, Cody's logging equipment breaking down, and they had to again borrow money from Amber's parents. The logging contract had a six-week holdback. Amber started work log scaling (how glad they were that she had gotten her unused scaling license now!) and brought home an inadequate paycheck every other week. Their Visa card could hardly hold the overload. To top it all off, Cody didn't get paid for his next contract, because the unscrupulous company declared bankruptcy (only to immediately start up again under another name, leaving several people unpaid and using their money. (*Jerks.*)

Cody sold his equipment at a loss to pay off their debts, giving up his dream of becoming a wealthy contractor. He took a job (with a more trustworthy company) for quality control of the wood being sorted and put in various decks on logging landings for shipping and selling. The highest grades of logs were destined for an overseas market. He quickly understood what they wanted and did a good job. The company promoted him to oversee the other quality control personnel. Soon his knowledge and skill, with most other aspects of logging, earned him the job of foreman over the five contractors working for the company. He now had the respect and appreciation that his work ethics had earned him. Sure, he still often drank too much, but he never drank 5:00 am to 5:00 pm. Job-related decisions and complications often extended into his "own time." He handled it, being direct, calling things as he saw them without worrying about being politically correct. He lived in the logging camp during the week and went home on weekends.

"Your husband needs you to pick him up at the hospital." The town's doctor phoned Amber. "He had some metal filings in his eye that I had to remove. You knew his other eye was glass, didn't you? He can't see with the temporary bandage on," he haltingly explained. By the next morning, Cody could take the bandage off and see good again. He wore glasses to protect the one eye he had left the next time he had to file anything.

Amber maintained their home and worked at her job. Since they were all used to living frugally, their savings grew and their bills were paid. They purchased a modest fixer-upper at the end of a dead end street, so they no longer had rent to pay. Carey and Cybil helped Amber build an addition to their home and make a backyard garden. They did well in school and graduated with honors. Carey could have made straight A's but found many things more interesting than schoolwork. Inventive and handy, he earned the nickname "MacGyver." He took several different jobs before he found the one that fit him best. Cybil earned scholarships and was made valedictorian at her graduation. She fulfilled one of her father's dreams by going on to college. Angela was working steady, doing well as a dental assistant. She took night classes for college and was making plans to marry. Cody and Amber were proud and grateful how their children had become loving responsible adults pursuing their own lives and careers.

# Chapter 22

Working in a sawmill yard as a piece scaler and weigh scaler, Amber found that the loaderman liked to joke around while waiting to spread more logs out for scaling. "I'm just making puppies until I can pick up the logs you scaled and can spread out another load." He laughed.

Though unfamiliar with the saying and implications of the term he'd used, Amber quickly admonished playfully, "You leave those dogs alone, now, Henry!" The other scalers howled with laughter.

When weigh scaling, part of the scaler's duty was to check and record the test weights of the four scale sections as the loader stopped on each of the sections and back again each morning. If the weight difference was over the Forest Service allowance (usually fifty kilograms), it had to be immediately fixed or reported to Forest Service before weighing truckloads of logs. When Amber arrived before opening time, she often shoveled snow or mud off the scale deck to help maintain correct weighing. This ensured the logs received an accurate *net* weight when the truck weighed back out emptied. The net weight was given an average cubic meter conversion for payment purposes to the contractors and for government stumpage tax. To get a conversion, a random sample load of logs was hand ("piece") scaled to find the actual cubic meters of pulp and sawable wood of each specie the load contained. After being multiplied by the net weight formula, the resulting conversion was applied to a given number of similar loads (i.e., hemlock, pine, spruce, or balsam with mainly pulp or sawable wood) that only needed to be weighed.

Government check scalers would occasionally make sure scaling was done accurately by hand scaling the same load the industry scalers had scaled. If there was over a 5 percent difference, the check scaler's scale replaced the disgraced original scaler's results. Most checkers would give the benefit of the doubt to a scaler who truthfully and reasonably saw a log differently. Very few scalers were careless or dishonest enough to lose their license to scale. Mills might try to influence scalers for getting lower grades and less volume to pay stumpage on, but if that happened, contractors would also unfairly receive less pay for their work. Amber wasn't really worried about the government, because she thought they wasted too many tax dollars, but she was conscientious to do a fair job of scaling for the working people involved.

Under pressure of early, long, irregular hours, broken down equipment, and the hazards of hauling heavy loads on often treacherous roads, the logging truck drivers could be impatient with Forest Service requirements. "Do you want cheese with that whine?" or "I'm teaching my dog to drive truck. He already knows how to whine," was common banter. The majority of the drivers were good natured with the scalers. Rules, however, had to be followed. Logs had to be properly timber-marked to indicate where the wood had been harvested.

Amber gave a weary driver (she knew he hauled from the same area continually) a can of paint. "I really have to go to the bathroom before I weigh your truck in."

When she came back, the proper timber marks had magically become easy to see. She weighed the truck in with a clear conscience. When weighing the empty truck back out, she casually remarked how a scaler could lose their license if they ever weighed an unmarked load. The driver always had well-marked loads from then on, and the situation was never mentioned. Amber was able to say that she'd never knowingly weighed an unmarked load.

If a careless driver raced onto the scale too fast, he was told how one scale house was demolished as a load overturned on an icy scale. The scalers barely escaped out the back door, and this scale house has no back door. Smart drivers grinned and drove onto the scale slower next time. Amber enjoyed the easy banter and friendliness that came with the job. The check scalers showed her friendliness and respect as well. She never felt like it was "too much information" when anyone chose to share some of their private lives and concerns with her. She listened with respect and didn't come across as judgmental.

Amber took a motherly interest in a young, new driver. "You've got to get some sleep and enough to eat to keep up the pace you're setting," she admonished as she sent her plug in lunch kit, with food inside, with him. He had confided some of his troubles on the job and how he wasn't finding time to get something hot to eat either. It was his first serious work so far away from home, family, and friends. At the end of the season, he said goodbye and thanked Amber for mothering him as he returned the lunch kit that enabled him to have hot food while logs were being loaded onto his truck. He was a real nice youngster that she would always remember fondly.

Cody was quite proud of Amber when she was hired to run the new scaling system for the same company he worked for. They were invited to house parties, dinners, and company get-togethers. Amber, still socially awkward, was fine as long as she wasn't expected to make any first moves at circulating among guests. Cody, after embarrassing himself in front of the big brass, learned to trust Amber's warnings if he were losing his common sense. He would happily head home with her before it was too late. They were becoming friends.

# Chapter 23

Tesley was still the home they planned to move back to eventually if work became available for them there. It would be nearer to where their children were living.

Amber was offered a job back in Budding. If her bosses had not hired (and promoted with higher pay) an arrogant, lazy, and irritating man over her, she probably would not have given her resignation to take the new job. The other scalers she worked with expressed their disappointment in her leaving and the new scaler taking over because they knew his reputation from the other scale house he'd worked at. They had to hire two more people to take her place when she left. The new man refused to go out on the water to count the bundles of logs in the ocean booms that had been part of her duties. It was too dangerous for him, and therefore the other scalers also. The unfit man might fall in if he attempted to jump from bundle to bundle inside the ocean's boom (chained together long logs, securely chained into rocks on the inlet's shore, floated around banded loads of similar specie and quality of logs) to get an accurate count for inventory. The tugboat operator would drop Amber off, leave for half an hour while she spray-painted a number on each bundle. Then pick her back up so she could check out the accuracy of inventory to be sold. Amber had found it fun and exciting to jump from bundle to bundle, occasionally disturbing a seal that was resting on one. When the wind and swirling water moved the bundles around, she still made it to all of them. Now the company would have to rely on the tugboat operator's original count. They would not have the extra proof for refuting alleged accounting inaccuracy occurring during storms. They would need to resort to creative ingenious inventions, not necessarily based on truth.

Cody and Amber's house sold quickly by accepting a down payment and a bit higher than rent monthly payment so the young family wouldn't need to go through a bank loan. All of Amber's moving expenses were paid by her new employers. She and Cody would still meet on most weekends. They would just have to travel a few hours each and meet at a motel. It would be a good relaxing way to go sightseeing where they knew moose and other wildlife hung out. The company had always given them two months off, with full pay, when logging shut down each spring. They figured it would be a workable arrangement. It went well, and soon Cody was back home in Tesley with Amber for the spring shut down.

Amber traveled from Tesley to Budding each day for her job. She needed an hour and a half traveling time in the morning to make sure she wouldn't be late even though the road was paved and no longer as winding as it had been the first time she traveled it. It made a long day, but she enjoyed her job. Cody began to have dinner ready for her when she arrived back home. She was thankful and amazed. He had turned out to be a good cook and enjoyed knowing it. The day was a long time ago when he opened a box of Kraft Dinner and boiled everything together like soup for the children when Amber was too sick to get out of bed. They both had a good laugh, though, when he thought baking soda would thicken gravy instead of corn starch or flour. He knew it was something white, but it bubbled and didn't taste right.

When Cody returned to work, his weekends were not often available for himself because he had to check landings. It was agreed that Amber could share the foreman's private living quarters and visit him at work. With at least a ten-hour drive, she'd usually leave Tesley early Saturday morning and travel back Sunday at least every other weekend (they had more time on long weekend holidays). By using three hours of banked time, she left work early one Friday and headed for Cody's camp, saving the extra time of traveling from Tesley.

Amber arrived at the logging camp late at night. No one noticed her car pull up and park. She quietly carried her suitcase inside the main camp. Silently she slipped into the foreman's private rooms. After freshening up in his bathroom and exchanging her traveling clothes for a nightgown, she went into the bedroom and closed the door gently. She crawled into his bed and snuggled into his warmth. She was almost asleep when his body began to react to her nearness. His hands started to roam over her body.

Suddenly Cody's entire body tensed. As if in a dream, that was no dream, he came awake with a start! "Who are you?" he hissed.

Amber laughed quietly. "Who do you want me to be?" she asked suggestively.

"Amber?" he sounded relieved, if a bit guilty. "How…when… you're here?" Then less talk and more action as their lips and bodies found each other.

They slept content until the alarm clock sounded, calling Cody to his job.

Amber quickly dressed to accompany Cody on his rounds to check the different landings and log decks. Then they had no more responsibilities, except to each other. They went back to the bunkhouse for lunch and watched the cook and camp attendant play "Spite and Malice." It was just like Skip-Bo, except played with two decks of real playing cards. They learned how to play, but soon got restless.

"Let's have a look at some mushroom buying stations. Our buckerman and faller pick and sell pine mushrooms on their weekends," Cody suggested. After a brief look and discussion with the buyers, they decided it would be fun to search for the mushrooms themselves. The lonely grader man Eric and his dog went with them into a pine and hemlock forest where the mushrooms should grow. They brought back what they found to the buyers. Half of what they found were poisonous or just worthless mushrooms. The few good ones they found got them hooked on mushroom finding adventures. They were warned about bears being a real danger if they didn't hear them coming and it was a good thing to have a dog with also.

"Don't quit your day job!" seasoned pickers laughed at their measly finds. They didn't offer any secrets how to find more. Their backpacks were filled with prime solid, fresh "button" mushrooms that had not opened into "flags" like most of the mushrooms that Cody and Amber found.

Gradually, Cody and Amber discovered how to check around the visibly big cowboy-hat-shaped white mushrooms flags (that were often wormy and rotten) for the more valuable "buttons." They became more adept at identifying the real from the lookalikes. Too bad they only had the weekends.

Cody had developed a keen sense of direction from his years of experience in hunting and hiking through the woods. Amber, though, could turn around to pick a mushroom and lose her way immediately. She paid more attention to where Cody was than to where they'd been, or were going, because he expected her to follow him. Voice contact ("Hello? Hello!") was a must for them *both* to find their way back—and it helped keep the bears away. Like old-time prospectors who caught "gold fever" by finding a few nuggets, they caught mushroom fever, by finding unexpected button mushrooms. In another year, they knew the exact areas to go back to when looking for the new fall harvest.

Every year, buyers set up for the pine pickers in the same area. It had gained the name everyone came to know as the "zoo." In its heyday, at least ten buying stations (tarp and plastic covered, wood frame shacks or portable store bought garages) were set up to compete for the pickers' mushrooms. Competition and the Japanese market kept the prices high enough that a really good, experienced picker could make a month's wage in a few days in a productive year. Many came to understand how possessive and secretive other pickers were of their patches. Stories of violence erupting between pickers who went to the same areas were common place.

If picked every three days, an area had more of a chance to remain secret by cleaning out all visible mushrooms. A new picker might assume none grew in that area. Cody and Amber still had to keep their day jobs, but if they had any vacation time, guess where they'd go!

Dennis, otherwise known as "Time Bomb," roamed many of the buyer's shacks in the sitting areas around the wood burning stoves where the pickers could warm up, sell their day's find, and socialize with each other. Dennis was extremely possessive of the pine mushroom patches in areas that he picked. There were rumors that he would gladly sugar a competitors gas tank or even attack those who picked in "his" patch.

Cody and Amber listened to the story he was telling a group of young rowdy pickers. "When I was in jail," he was saying, "there was a big thug who bothered me once too often. Next time in the exercise yard, I found a good-sized rock to put in the sock I'd put in my pocket. Without anyone seeing me, I whapped the thug full force in the back of his head. Then I walked calmly away, emptied my sock, and stuck it back in my pocket. Put the bastard in a coma! Ain't nobody gonna mess with me. Didn't leave no evidence either."

Amber, seeing the look of uneasy disbelief crossing some of the new pickers faces, piped up, "Remind me to stay your friend and not your enemy, Dennis. You know they could get DNA evidence from your sock if they found fibers in the back of his head. Did you get rid of the sock?"

The buyer chimed in. "Cody and Amber were in your patch today, you know," he teased.

"Don't even joke about that if you want them to live to sell to you!" Time Bomb threatened. Small of stature, Dennis enjoyed being scary and strange.

# Chapter 24

After years of traveling back and forth to be with each other, Amber was offered a newly made scaling job. She could live at camp with Cody. He convinced her to quit her job and take the new one. Their son and his girlfriend could live in their house in Tesley. They could be together more.

It turned out to be a great job for Amber, just scaling the wasted ends of logs that were bucked off to make the remaining log a more valuable product for selling mainly to overseas markets. A large stamp hammer (with the metal timber mark letters and numbers welded onto it) was provided for her to hammer the mark into the ends of each log that was left. It was necessary to hit it hard and just right to have all the mark to show up. She and the buckermen became friends who joked around with each other developing a sense of "ha, ha." She compiled the volumes at the end of the day and sent the results to the company office so the government would be paid stumpage for the wasted part of the tree as well as the final product. Then she enjoyed her leisure and the room and board provided at camp.

"Men didn't have it so bad," she decided. "Sure they might work hard away from home, but when the day was done, their only requirement was to eat a fully prepared meal with a choice variety of salads, desserts, milk, coffee, tea, and juices. Full laundry facilities were available, but they didn't even have to wash their own bedding. Their rooms were cleaned and their beds remade each week. Royalty couldn't have it much better, and it was all part of the paid package!" Amber found lots of spare time for sewing quilts, crafts, and entertainment like reading, playing cards, or watching TV.

If the mess hall was filled up, Cody and Amber took their dinners to their private rooms. Right after dinner, Cody would gather with the contractors to plan the next day's logging, road building, bridge maintenance, or trucking strategies. The grader man (Eric) and Cody would often continue to drink heavily at Eric's trailer after the plans were made. Amber learned not to wait for the meeting to be over but kept busy until she went to sleep without Cody.

Cody and Amber toured the landings on the weekends to assess the amount of logs decked for loading the logging trucks. The trucks would need to be organized and scheduled so the drivers would not be lined up and waiting for each other. The loaderman would be kept busy digging into the decks of wood to load trucks the next day as they came and went to their assigned landings. If an extremely rotten log had been accidently decked, Cody or Amber would brightly paint it so the loaderman could quickly identify and discard it instead of uselessly loading it. Amber wrote down Cody's estimate for each landing and contractor's site. Cody phoned the information into the office so Monday morning start up could be organized by knowing how many trucks were needed at each landing.

Often the early-morning tour brought them above the clouds, high up the mountainside with a breathtaking view of the valley below. Logging trucks would have to be able to travel to these landings to pick up the decked logs. Bridges had been built across streams and needed to be inspected. Checks were made to see that the bales of straw and landscaping cloth were doing their job of preventing erosion of the soil. The bridge timbers needed to be strong and stay firmly in place. Dump trucks of crushed rock needed to be spread over some muddy areas of roads before logging trucks were able to haul. "No one," mused Amber, "would be aware of how much planning, overseeing, work, and details logging required if they were not involved in it."

Cody made quick decisions with apparent ease. When a slash burn got out of control and the company's forester in charge quavered over the price of a water bomber, Cody advised quick control. He assured him it would certainly be much cheaper than allowing a large forest fire to start up by taking a chance.

Amber remembered the slash burn Cody had taken her to before they were married. "It's nature's way of renewing the forest," he had explained. "Stupid Greenpeacers haven't done their homework or experienced things firsthand." She had to agree that government often made decisions not based on facts or smart usability but made useless rules that were never tested by the ones making them. They should have to work side by side for just one week with those their rules affected before making them. Some rules were good, but then everyone should have to keep them without some special groups being exempt.

Cody and Amber were working well together and the company was pleased with the extra help Cody was provided by her being there on the weekends. Cody still vented some of his frustrations out on Amber, but not often. Oscar, one of the contractors, overheard Cody raging at Amber with obscenities and ridicule. Later on, he engaged Amber in private friendly conversation.

"It's a woman's own fault," he inserted into the topic being discussed, "if she accepts any kind of abuse from a man by not standing up for herself and allowing it."

"Oh, is it her fault also if a man is of a domineering and self-centered personality? If he's been brought up to think it's all right or funny to show a lack of respect to those closest to him? Sometimes one has to consider the source no matter how much they *so* do not accept it or never will. If a woman is bossy, lazy, and an untidy pack rat, is it the man's fault?" Amber questioned his reasoning. "Perhaps mutual respect started by one of them would be the best solution." She was tired of being blamed for Cody's tendencies.

"You do have some spark when someone is actually listening, don't you?" Oscar grinned. "Here I thought you were milk toast personality! I suppose it wouldn't make sense for two idiots to be tearing each other apart." He wisely steered the conversation in another direction.

Later, Oscar made sure Cody could overhear him speaking with other men and saying, "If a man wants any kind of respect, he should be able to show respect to those around him."

Cody puzzled over the look Oscar gave him, thinking, *Sure he talked roughly back and forth with the men, but they showed each other respect in what counted. Men called each other dumb head, stupid, and worse all the time with swear words mixed in, letting off steam.* He didn't realize he could dish it out better than he could take it, especially with Amber.

"Something is wrong with my stomach," Amber complained. "Do you feel this?" She placed Cody's hand on her lower abdomen. It was swollen, but she hadn't gained weight. She couldn't have a change of life pregnancy with her tubes tied either.

"Go to a doctor," Cody absently suggested.

She did and was asked how old she was. Apparently she should expect to be losing her shape and gaining weight at the old age of forty something. Amber went back to work, ready to believe it was all in her mind. The thing kept growing. Her back started hurting to where she could hardly get in and out of a vehicle to do her job.

They returned to Tesley for the Christmas holidays. Amber went back to a doctor for a second look, asking for something for her back pain. This time the doctor felt the growth that had gotten big enough to cause pressure on her spine. An ultra sound was ordered immediately. Surgery was scheduled within the week by cancelling someone else's. Though aware that the doctor was taking it unusually seriously, Amber was glad that at least she wasn't a hypochondriac.

Cody continually partied over the holidays without her. Amber angrily thought, "Even if its cancer like what killed my aunt and grandma, I'm tired enough that I'd almost rather die than have an endless future dealing with drunken abuse." She told herself that she was glad Cody was leaving to go back to work and she could drive herself into Budding for the operation. She didn't admit that she was pouting.

Cody resisted the thoughts that came into his mind as he made the long drive back to camp. If the growth was cancerous, he could lose Amber for good. She had said he really didn't care about her anyhow, just how it affected his own selfish wants. She was only a convenience to him and he could easily find another.

He went back to work as usual but was drinking more than ever with Eric after the work day. He was accused of drinking on the job when one of the new rigid managers visited and smelled stale alcohol on him the next day. In spite of the other manager vouching for him, he was sent packing without consideration.

Meanwhile, a benign fibroid tumor was taken out of Amber. Pressure causing her backache was gone. She was surprised to see Cody walk into her hospital room.

"I couldn't stand being away from you and worrying about you. I could hardly eat or sleep. So I quit to be with you," Cody stretched the truth. When he applied for unemployment insurance, the real story came out. They were both out of work. Amber chose not to go back to camp because they had another scaler to replace her. She recuperated from her operation quickly even at her "old age." They had to depend on their savings account to get by.

# Chapter 25

Cody quit drinking for a year to prove to himself that he wasn't a dysfunctional alcoholic. Though Amber enjoyed an occasional drink before, she also quit to encourage his decision. He had terrible mood swings and wasn't easy to live with, but he stuck to it. Amber explained to him that she'd read that people could have "dry drunks" if they'd been used to drinking quite a bit. He resented that information. Some of his friends encouraged him by the respect they showed him when he refused a drink. "Right on, man" or "I respect your decision" was a common comment by those who didn't have their own excessive drinking habit. The buddies that refused to let go of their attempts to get him drinking again looked more like pathetic losers to his sober state of mind…even when they brought up the song lyrics "It's 'Honey, do this' and 'Honey, do that.' You're not much fun since I quit drinking" to insinuate that he'd be bored by his wife and sober friends now and had to tow their lines. He'd made the decision to quit for a year and stuck to it. Gradually he had a harmless glass of wine with meals. He had a social beer now and again. Sure that he was in control of his intake of alcohol, he enjoyed having a stiff drink now and again. Alcohol didn't bother keeping its foot in the door. It walked slowly back in.

The cycle was repeating itself. "You stupid bitch," Cody railed at Amber in his mood swing rage.

"What you mean is, love of my life, my precious, beautiful, kind, wonderful wife whom I adore," Amber teased, giving him what she thought was a better choice of words again.

When she thought Cody became too demanding, Amber went into an Edith and Archie Bunker routine that amused Cody. "Yes, dear, right away, Archie." She shuffled around running to obey his commands and blinking blankly with pretended confusion on her face as if the roared obscenities went over her head. "What would you like me to do now, dear?" They could both laugh at themselves.

Cody and Amber were both mainly unemployed. Winter had been cold, long, and dreary. Their children ran into personal problems, but Amber was a failure at helping them when they needed her. A good friend died of cancer, another friend rejected Amber for saying the wrong thing at the wrong time. She felt like the best thing she could do for others was to stay away. God wasn't answering her prayers. Cody's friend died of kidney failure, Amber's brother died in a car accident, and her father died of a heart attack. The faith to move God's will eluded her. Things didn't seem quite real anymore. She started to look for deeper meanings in everyday things. Many things seemed to have a double meaning. She experienced deep sadness, hopelessness, and mood swings. Cody and her friends could tell she was acting strange. She thought God should be able to show her why things were happening the way they were. She must have done something to deserve what was happening around her.

Good intentioned people flooded her with self-help books and how to get results through greater faith books. Apparently she didn't have an inferiority complex but was just plain inferior. She watched a television show that meant something to her and seemed like more than a coincidence, the way it related to what she was struggling with. She wasn't hearing voices, but when she said the television spoke to her, Cody had her committed to the hospital mental ward.

She was given a shot of something and put into a fully padded room with a monitoring camera looking down on her. She told the camera that she was sorry for everything she had done wrong, but she wasn't sorry for still believing in God. She woke up in a bed in a private room. She was shown films that were meant to be therapeutic toward getting her to open up about what might have caused some of her mental condition. She took the pills that were to correct her chemical imbalance and depression. She followed instructions but kept her thoughts to herself. After a few days, they released her with the little pink pills she would need to keep taking. They controlled the highs and lows to the point that she was starting to realize genuine feelings and reactions were missing.

She got hired to do some scaling. Those around them quit getting sick and dying. The things she had worried about seemed to be getting better. She was able to quit taking her pills and felt more normal again. She wasn't about to tell anyone how rainbows or beautiful sunsets spoke to her of God's love, just in case they'd think she was hearing voices. Sometimes she wished she could have Cody committed for his uncontrolled anger and drinking, though.

Amber found the part-time work wasn't enough to support their lifestyle. They were dipping further into what was left of their savings. The bottom had dropped out of their investments. "Buy low, sell high" had turned into "sell now or have nothing left." Much as they tried, jobs just were not available with the recession hitting the logging industry.

# Chapter 26

"We'll go camp back up north for August and September and pick pine mushrooms!" Cody had a brainstorm. They acquired a dog and bought a used tent trailer. They packed up food and supplies and headed for the adventure. The tent trailer was so cold without a working heater that when the weather turned bad, Amber heated rocks in the campfire. She wrapped the rocks in tinfoil then in a towel and brought them inside to bed so they could be warm enough to get to sleep. They were finding enough mushrooms to pay for their gas expense and enjoying the fresh air and exercise.

They were befriended by Norm and Edie, a couple who were seasoned pickers. Every fall they travelled from their home in Alberta (where they had settled after many years of travelling adventures that included odd jobs, all types of mushroom picking, and gold mining) to pick pine mushrooms in BC because they so thoroughly enjoyed it. Through their amazing generosity and instructions, Cody and Amber became much better campers and pickers. They were shown how to identify and dry chanterelle, sweet tooth, boletes, and other edible mushrooms that could be found as they were looking for the pine mushrooms.

Norm and Edie decided to leave early to beat the coming snowstorms. They offered their trailer addition shack with the wood heater to Cody and Amber to finish the season. The small plastic-walled, rainproof shelter with an airtight heater made their airy tent trailer warm up considerably when they parked up against it. They could pick in the rain and come back to camp to dry out and warm up. They made their expenses and some extra.

"A bear! A bear, bear, bear, chasing me!" Young native Jonah, exhausted and almost hysterically breathless, pounded on the door of Cody and Amber's camp in the middle of the night. They saw no bear, but let Jonah inside and made coffee to share while Jonah told his tale.

"I was in the middle of the best patch of mushrooms ever. The mossy ground was white with pine mushrooms. It was a whole village of them! My pack had at least fifty pounds in it and the sun was starting to set when I looked the bear in his eyes. I knows you not supposed to run from bear but couldn't help myself. I leaves my pack where it was. I run, run, run and keep on running. Know I'm lost, but hear the bear keep following. Finally, I have to quit running. I try to think where the way out of the trees might be. I find the road, but hear bear again and am running and running and running again until here I am. You take me to where I camp. I get the rest of my things. You take me where I can get a ride out of here. I ain't never going picking again, ever!" Jonah declared. "Let the bears eat you honkies, but not me!" Jonah knew he was totally entitled to the help they willingly gave him, because some of their ancestors were said to be unfair to some of his ancestors. He had no idea unfairness was practiced by all races at times and many races received no compensations for past harmful history any more than credit also for any good they had done.

Bear attacks did happen. A human skeleton was found mutilated in the forest with a deadly pointed stick through the center of his torso. It was assumed he had impaled himself as he ran from a bear through the woods in a blind panic (or perhaps an overzealous picker had attacked him first). Only the foolish think there are no dangers deep in the bush. Even experienced people panicked, got lost for days and died of exposure, or had accidents or been attacked. Common sense, good luck, and their dog Feisty were on Cody and Amber's side. Cody always made sure to head out of the woods two or more hours before dark. Cody planned to build a fire and stay where they were until daylight if they ever did get lost near dusk. He told Amber to stay put instead of looking for him if she lost voice contact, he had a better chance of finding her than she had of looking for him and getting further lost. She hollered her head off "Hello" a few different times before his answering calls helped her find her way back to a safer distance from the only one who would be able to lead her back to their vehicle.

In the following years, Cody and Amber had a similar shelter to Norm and Edie's, a few hundred feet away for their own small, new to them, house trailer. It was a custom to camp near each other. They went out picking their own patches each day and sold their mushrooms. They came back to enjoy their evenings by having a few drinks together. The fresh air and exercise made them tired before the drinking got out of control and they would retire to their own camps for dinner and the rest of the evening. Norm, Edie, and Cody were born storytellers, sharing past experiences and telling jokes. They watched the beaver family in the pond next to their camps. The baby beaver made them laugh at the way it nudged its mother to nurse until the mother relented. Gradually the baby was taught how to pull a small branch through the water to their beaver hut. The observers became fast friends who looked forward to seeing each other, and the beavers, every fall.

At the end of one season, Cody decided to chance leaving their trailer at camp only to find it vandalized and burnt when they returned the next season. Cody assumed it was probably a competitive picker or a native that claimed they had special entitlement to everything everywhere. They spent a rough night camping in Norm and Edie's addition since they hadn't arrived yet. Then they went to buy lumber nails and plastic from the nearest town to build a rough shelter.

Cody and Amber finished their camp meal and played cards before going to bed. The rain poured against their shack, but the airtight wood heater kept them warm and dry. Rain gear would be a necessity to go out picking the next day, but getting soaked was still inevitable. The rain was much needed! It would help get the mushrooms growing and save them a trip for wash water. Nailed on eaves troughs channeled the rain water from the roof into their water containers. For at least a month, they would live in the rough wood frame structure with the plywood floor and plastic walls and roof. A sheet hung between their eight-by-eight bedroom and the main eight-by-sixteen living area. Their faithful dog Feisty slept under the camp table on her blanket and pillow. Their bed was an old bring your own bed frame that normally came with an air mattress. However, Cody screwed down plywood over top of it to posts securing it to the floor. (Anything that could be easily taken and packed away, typically got stolen). Amber washed the covers of several couch cushions she salvaged from discarded couches. The cushions were recovered and provided the bottom mattress under their four-inch foamy that they brought with every year. (Surprisingly, no one stole them when they left them stored inside garbage bags to protect them from mice every year. Stove pipes and stoves, however, could seldom be hidden well enough not to be gone if left behind). A stainless steel bucket with a lid held water heated on the wood stove for washing up. Wood-framed metal screens rested on a frame above the heat so mushrooms could be spread out and dried for those they wanted to keep and preserve. Tubs with lids (to protect the contents from mice or other creatures) contained most of the supplies they needed for the duration, but a trip to a nearby town was often used to restock fresh food and drinks. The local garbage dump was labeled the "hardware store" where many campers comfortably furnished their dwellings with salvaged items. "Sour grapes," maybe, but they preferred their shack to a fancy motor home with all the comforts of a house on wheels. Besides, their travel load was heavy enough with supplies and their quad.

"Time Bomb", Dennis, often visited with Norm and Edie, and Cody and Amber when they came to the buyers to sell their day's harvest at the zoo. One year, he was on a peanut butter kick, extolling it as a totally balanced and complete food source. Then he was keeping a journal of the food he ate each day and recording samples of bowel movements associated with the food. Next, he declared his brown eyes were turning blue from the cleansing diet he was on.

"Yeah, Dennis"—most humored him as they pretended to examine his eyes—"they're not as brown as they were."

After the finish of one season, Time Bomb was working on the bus he used as his home. He had a good fire in his wood stove for warmth. He'd gotten diesel all over himself as he fixed the irksome leak. He went back inside to stoke his fire and warm up…and burst into flame himself. He was brought to the hospital but never recovered. Many pickers remember Time Bomb rather fondly, retelling stories of him and other characters who had shown up at the "zoo" during mushroom season for many years.

Flocks of new pickers with dreams of making the old time money found themselves stranded and starving during a bad pine season year when dry weather conditions killed the crop. The kindhearted shantyman organization set up soup kitchens and set up a water tap for the zoo people. Starry eyed dreamers had no idea how much work, survival talents, and knowledge would be required when they descended on the mushroom picking scene. Very similar to those in history who were unprepared in failing to find gold in the gold rush times.

Sid, a skinny unkempt character with dreadlocks and tattered clothes, stumbled drunkenly into Cody and Amber's camp where they were enjoying a relaxing drink outside after the day's picking. Sid wanted a drink, but Amber sensed he would have an unquenchable thirst if they began sharing any booze with him.

"I'll fix you a tea or coffee with cookies if you'd like to visit, but we don't share our booze. It's too hard to replace," Amber stated as she offered him a camp chair. Disappointment showed on Sid's face as he accepted the offer of the chair and tea and cookies.

"You remind me of my parents. They are always telling me to be reliable and responsible and quit doing drugs and drinking. God can give me a new and better life they say." Sid extended his middle finger to the sky. "This is what I think of God," he said. Then he jumped up, turned around, and exposed his painfully scared buttocks. "God did this to me! I was laying by a campfire to stay warm and almost burnt up!" Sid let go a stream of vulgarity. "I'll never believe in God!"

"The god who led you, *yourself*, to do that is better known as Satan, who comes to steal, kill, and destroy. The Bible says he is the god of this world. Most gods people tell me they don't believe in are not the loving Creator, wise Father they never got to know." Amber was shocked at his display but couldn't resist giving her opinion.

Sid continued to visit, amusing them with the tale of how his dreadlocks rotted off before they would get much longer. He accepted some of the extra clothing that Amber wanted to get rid of so they wouldn't have to bring it back with them. He had another cup of tea. He would visit them again occasionally when he could stomach more tea.

Cody and Amber always made sure they had enough of a safety net for being able to survive the travel expense of getting back home for unreasonably low prices and unproductive years. Mushroom exporters had formed a mafia type union to force buying prices down, as well as a lowered demand for the supposed aphrodisiac in pine mushrooms that Viagra could replace. Drugs and alcohol spawned riots between pickers and buyers when the prices dropped overnight. A group of pickers poured out baskets of mushrooms and stomped them into the ground. They tipped over a broken down car and set fire to it. When they ran out of money for their addictions, they went back to picking again for any price. Other diehard pickers continued to sell because if they didn't, someone else would find their patches and be the ones to sell. Cody and Amber lost some of their best spots by going home early when the prices dropped too low.

# Chapter 27

"You should try picking morel mushrooms," a buyer suggested to Cody. Soon he and Amber were camping near a last year's forest fire area late in the spring. They were fighting mosquitoes and living in a tent. Cody built a rough kitchen shelter, strengthening the support posts he cut from the burn with his power saw by digging a deep hole for them to be put in before filling the dirt back in snuggly with extra rocks. Amber was still impressed by his know-how and capabilities in the great outdoors. The tarps kept them dry but far from mosquito free. Amber tried to keep mostly covered so she wouldn't have to use as much bug repellent as Cody did. Hiking, picking, and packing mushrooms was hard, dirty work, but good exercise. Having a quad to get further in the bush and to pack their mushrooms back out was a plus. They had never worked so hard for so little money. It was the thrill of finding a patch of mushrooms that no one else was in that always gave them the excitement. Down on their hands and knees, they carefully cut and harvested firm morels that were over two inches high with a quarter inch or less stem. If it were a thick patch, it would be worth going back in a couple days to reharvest the area.

Another perk to picking morels was to travel to different parts of BC and Alberta, or even to the Yukon and Northwest Territories where there had been a previous year's fire. They got to see and know different places they had never seen before. Traveling and working together, setting up camps and enjoying the great outdoors became a way of life. They picked where herds of bison roamed. They experienced their first taste of the delicious pickerel fish. They were drawing closer together and gaining survival skills.

Amber had her usual pack on and was bent over picking a nice patch of morels not far from Cody. Suddenly something let out an ungodly shriek and dove right into her back, knocking her over. Ospreys are very protective of their nests and Amber had, unknowing, been picking too close to it. Cody heard the shriek and saw the swooping thunk as it attempted to attack Amber and fly away. At first he thought she'd been hurt, but the pack had protected her from its claws, wings, and beak. It gave another shriek as Amber lay where she'd been knocked, laughing in unbelief. She picked her way closer to where Cody had been picking. Later that day, she pointed out a small rabbit that thought it was hidden under a burnt log's camouflage. More than once, grouse flew suddenly up from their nests to startle them. Sometimes the birds would just stare at the intruders in the hope they would not be seen. Anytime they saw a mother with an early hatch, it would pretend to be wounded to lure the danger away from her chicks. These were experiences that money could not buy and Amber loved it. She thought it was priceless and awesome to be so intimate with nature. Cody enjoyed it every bit as much but was a more seasoned, less impressed, experienced bushman.

They were having a good day of picking far enough away from each other that Cody didn't see what was in the patch where Amber was picking. A Happy Birthday balloon lay at rest after escaping someone else's party. It *was* Amber's birthday and it was one of the best patches she had ever stumbled into. She called Cody over to help her pick it. They marveled at the birthday gift complete with the party balloon. She just had to take it back down the mountain and home with her when the season was over. Who would ever believe them if they didn't have the evidence to prove what they'd found in the middle of an uninhabited mountain.

"I bet we could make it through that gully if we put rocks and logs enough to get our quad across to that other mountainside. We'd have a better chance of finding ground that's not already picked." Cody formulated his plan, and he and Amber filled in enough rocks and logs that Cody and the quad made it across. Amber followed with Feisty until he stopped for them to get back onboard. When they came back with a full load, another picker met them at the other side of the makeshift bridge. He had been looking for a way to take his motorcycle up the mountainside. He chuckled as he thanked them for the bridge. At least they'd had one day without the constant competition of other pickers. They were getting by.

## Feisty

As soon as the pickup was being loaded up to go on another mushroom picking trip, Feisty, their half bear dog, half cattle dog, would make sure she wouldn't be left behind. No matter if the tailgate were up or down, Feisty would be in the back of the truck, laying on the highest container. She understood "get out of the way" but wasn't going to give up going back to where she knew she certainly must belong.

When she could run free in the bush through the trees, Feisty proved to be a superb addition to mushroom hunting. No animals could get close to her masters without her interference. Feisty had unbridled character for a dog. She chased a ball happily with extraordinary energy. At last she got tired of bringing it back to have Cody throw it for her again and again. She walked alongside Cody for a while, and then, looking up as if to say "Your turn," she tossed the ball down a ravine and waited for her master to get the ball this time. "Get the ball, Feisty," only made Feisty look like she was grinning with a gleam in her eyes.

Feisty loved to bark at squirrels and circle through the bush. She kept returning to her masters as if she wanted to make sure she had cleared all danger out of their paths. The only time she remained quiet was when they caught wind of a smelly bear. The bear never was seen close to Cody and Amber, so they figured Feisty was quietly running interference.

Feisty stood like she was riding shotgun on the back of their quad when she was allowed to ride without a leash. If she decided to jump off and chase through the bush to follow a scent, she caught up at breakneck speed, slurping up drinks of water in puddles without breaking her stride.

Feisty strongly believed in giving everyone opportunity to pet her at any sociable setting. She snuck to the younger pickers campfire instead of keeping guard outside her masters' tent when they retired for the night. She made friends with a young girl who enthused that Feisty "was the nicest dog she ever met."

Feisty was not an obedient dog, but the spirit and enthusiasm that poured from her almost made up for it. After she dug out some of the neighbors' plants and took home some solar lights (Amber attempted to repay the expense), she was tied up to a long dog run. Feisty would get loose and her collar would be destroyed. They caught her in action when she thought they weren't watching. She was walking backward until her leash was stretched out. Then she started shaking and pulling her head backward until the collar slipped past her neck and over her ears right over her small head. As soon as her head was out, Feisty went after her collar with a vengeance. She crunched up the clasp and chewed through the collar making double sure it couldn't be used again. They were forced to use a chain choke collar. Alas, Feisty's head was smaller than her neck, unless it was cinched up tighter when she pulled. It took many years before she understood she wouldn't be tied if she just stayed home when told.

By trial and error, they learned that only strong chains could keep Feisty safely cross tied in the back of the truck. She eagerly assisted the chaining up process knowing it meant she'd be included in a trip. She chewed anything she could reach and pretended to lurch at passing traffic (knowing from experience that the cross chain would hold her inside the truck box), barking incessantly. A muzzle only seemed to turn her into a ventriloquist, inciting her to be more determined to tear it off if at all possible. As Feisty got older, they almost quit using the muzzle to avoid her frenzy. The moment the truck stopped, she would lay down, quietly behaved, and rest. When a policeman insisted they put Feisty in a dog cage instead of cross tying her, Feisty went berserk. She ripped up the pillow and shirt meant to calm her and chewed up the hard plastic cage until her mouth was bleeding and she almost got out. Both her masters pitied her and went back to cross tying her safely. Amber was sure if another police saw the cage, they would have to agree it was the only humane thing to do.

Feisty hit the deck each time the truck entered a tunnel, scared and quiet. As soon as they emerged, she'd be up and eagerly barking and lurching at oncoming vehicles again. It made her masters (who were actually her servants) wonder if she had once almost got run over when she used to chase vehicles, and the tunnels reminded her of that.

# Chapter 28

After selling their mushrooms, morel pickers would often visit together and have a beer or drink. They were from such a variety of different backgrounds. Successful professionals, vagrants, pensioners, and adventurers parked next to each other near the picking area where the previous year's forest fire produced morels. Rich, poor, honest, thieves, tidy, filthy, friendly and outgoing, or reserved and contrary, they all had their reasons to be picking. From the beautiful state of the art motor homes to tenters with campfires to those who slept in their barely mobile vehicles, the campers settled.

Cody and Amber's habit to pick morels was to bring along an airtight wood stove, propane camp stove, folding table and chairs, ice chests (digging a hole in the ground and covering the ice chest there with a tarp kept it cooler longer), power saw, axe, tent and tarps, and anything else they thought was a necessity. Amber cleaned up and cooked dinner each day after picking. Cody relaxed, having a drink with the other pickers visiting their camp, making an occasional comment to her about what she should get done. She was often already started on what he instructed her to do as she laughed at him. "Man, am I ever lucky to have you tell me what to do, or I'd just stand here wondering, wouldn't I?" When she pointed out that she had already done, or was doing, what he wanted, he would laugh enough to make her wonder if he was just pulling her chain all along.

One of the pickers kept staring at Amber from whatever area of the camp he was at. When he introduced himself to Cody and Amber, he shook and then held Amber's hand much longer than necessary.

"A woman has such soft and gentle hands," he said as he tried to caress her work roughened fingers. Amber was creeped out more than flattered by his attention and was glad Cody stayed near. Her hands might have been almost soft once, but even picking with gloves on, they had become very rough and stained. She was relieved when he left their camp, but he continued to stare at her from his truck where he slept and camped.

That night, Cody asked for a backrub. "With your soft, gentle hands," he said chuckling. "Actually your sandpaper hands feel pretty good if you don't rub too hard. Kind of takes the scales off my skin."

# Chapter 29

When morel season was over for the year, Cody received a phone call from one of the past company managers, who had also been his friend. Would Cody consider overseeing the logging right-of-way for a mining company? It would be in the Fort Nelson area of BC, almost extending to the Alberta border. Cody accepted. Since they were just getting by in picking mushrooms, it seemed a godsend.

Amber helped him pack his truck with everything he might need at the work camp. She promised to meet him at the Fort Nelson motel for a visit if he phoned her and told her he had some time off. Cody was kept busy with his duties, building bridges and roads, and overseeing the logging. He called Amber several times, assuring her that everything was going well. The roads were snowy and icy by the time he had time off to meet her at the motel in Fort Nelson.

Bravely, Amber studied a map and planned her day-long drive. She looked forward to meeting Cody at the motel he named. She took the road that looked the shortest on the map but found herself desperately trying to stay on the road. It seemed to have no other traffic, probably because it was so poorly maintained. When she came to a crossroad, beside an abandoned garage, she didn't know which way to turn and she had little gas left. She studied the map again. She could freeze to death in the middle of nowhere if her decision to turn right was wrong. With relief, she made it to a gas station. The attendant told her how far away she was from her destination, surprised that she had made it through the back road safely. He pointed to just up the road, where turning left would put her on the main road to Fort Nelson. It was a straight shot from there right to the motel. Cody was waiting and happy to see her pull into the motel. She clung to him in relief. The next day they watched a dog sled race for entertainment. After the brief time of "Honeymooning" (as Cody labeled it), Amber stayed to the main road and had a more relaxing drive back to Tesley. When the contract finished, Cody joined her back there.

Back when they were both making good money, they had invested in some mining stocks. After several attempts at buying low and selling high, they realized they had actually bought high. Their main stock holdings had to be sold at a loss before they entirely fell off the market. No use crying over spilt milk when they could still go mushroom picking, when no more jobs showed up.
"I pick here every fall," John, a friendly pine mushroom picker, said. "Then I go to Fort Nelson to drive logging truck on the ice roads. They're looking for log scalers at the mills right now." He gave Cody and Amber company phone numbers to call. Amber phoned and sent her résumé. She was hired and given a date to start.
Cody told her that rent was out of the world there, and it might not be worth working and paying the rent. She decided to phone the Fort Nelson newspaper and place an add about a quiet working woman looking for a place to rent during winter log hauling season. She had a few responses and chose the best one. All she needed was provided in the pretty, newly single, woman's home. She had her own bedroom and could share the kitchen, living room, laundry facilities, and bathroom.
Amber didn't mind living on her own. Depending on the push for log inventory, she worked five to seven days a week. She could hardly believe what the good-paying job paid for overtime hours. She joined the gym for extra exercise and walked around town and did some shopping for entertainment but turned down invitations for dates, no matter how platonically they were offered. Cody remained at their home in Tesley, taking care of himself and Feisty. She and Cody talked often on the phone. She told him she'd gotten to see a couple of their mushroom picking friends—John, driving logging truck, and Harvey, who was operating a processor. One of her bosses had taken her for a tour where the logging was done so she would

have a better understanding of the necessity for ice roads across swamps and rivers. He explained, as they drove over a frozen river, that by spring, the large reinforcing logs would be reduced to toothpicks, by the ice and motion of the river beneath.

Amber became friends with a lady truck driver, Lois. One weekend they drove to the well-known Liard Hot Springs in Amber's car. Warmly dressed, they walked down the wooden walkway to the change rooms, stripped down to their bathing suits, and quickly went into the warm water. The steamy water had every fern and plant covered heavily with sparkly white frost. It was even more magnificent than the postcards displayed. There were cement benches under the water in the pool to sit on whenever they got tired of exploring the warmer and cooler areas of the pools. The upper pool was blocked off because of bear attacks. Only one other couple shared the pool with them. They shared that winter was the best time to enjoy the hot spring with less crowds and more beauty to enjoy. Lois and Amber felt like they were turning into prunes before they reluctantly left to have something to eat at the Toad Crossing cafe. The entire ceiling and most of the walls were covered in baseball caps of various colors and captions. The adventure was worth the time the trip took. Amber looked forward to going again, even if she had to make the trip by herself.

The next few years seemed to fly by, repeating themselves. To work only from mid-October to April, as long as the ice roads lasted, fit perfectly into the mushroom seasons. Then the mill shut down and so did the scaling. It was back to Tesley to look for work again.

Cody got a short job falling trees. He came home dog tired until he got back into shape. They were getting older, and work was getting harder to do and to find. If they could only get by until they could receive their pensions.

# Chapter 30

Cody had bucked up a good dead tree for their winter firewood supply, and Amber helped split and load it into the back of the pickup. The patchwork of tree plantations, old growth forests, logging, bush roads, hills, and snow-peaked mountains seemed to have no end. Hunting season traveling expense was justified by gathering firewood.

"See those moose tracks? They cross this gully to that mountain. It's a good place to hunt." Cody drove slowly up the road looking for signs, hoping to see moose or deer. They had gotten a group moose draw and had bought their tags for deer also. The corner of his eye caught a dark shape crossing the road farther up. "Did you see that?" he asked Amber. "Maybe it was a moose or deer!" He was excited, but she shook her head.

As he drove up the road toward where he'd seen it, Amber squealed, "There it is! A moose. You can see its horn paddles on either side of that big fir tree… It thinks it's hiding!"

Cody grabbed his gun and bullets while he tried to focus in on what Amber saw. "Where? Oh yeah, there it is…hot damn!" He quietly opened his door, easing out of the truck trying to calm himself. He crept along, loading his gun, and aimed the gun scope on the peaking moose as it made its move to escape over the hillside. It was stopped by the bullet and dropped instantly. Convinced that it was his normal clean shot, he lowered his gun. Suddenly the moose was struggling to get up again, desperate to run from the dangerous thing that was taking its life. Another shot tore into the moose and it was over.

Cody never liked to see an animal suffer, but he was always thankful to have moose meat. With Amber's help, he gutted the moose. His shots were good, not destroying any of the meat. They tied a rope to drag it down the hill with his truck. They unloaded their firewood to get later and winched the moose into the back of the pickup. Thank God for moose meat once again. They would hang and skin it when they got it home. With the cold weather, three or more days and they would get it butchered. Some of the fat would be cut off first to feed the wild birds that entertained them on their sundeck. They did have a bit of wild meat in their freezer, so Amber would pressure can it for camping supplies. They would replenish their freezer with the new meat. They had everything they needed and could also fill some of their wants. Too soon though, law-abiding hunters were forbidden to hunt moose, while certain special groups slaughtered and sold more than they made use of whenever they wanted, without fear of being disciplined for their abuse. It was hard for them not to resent different laws for different people. Shouldn't everyone be given equal treatment and be shown the same respect?

Amber again found work in Budding and traveled back and forth each day. Cody and Feisty went mushroom picking on their own when Amber had to work. Whenever she could, she took her vacation time to join them. She gladly drove for hours to get the excitement that picking always gave her.

Back when the children were small, Amber had struggled to grow a good garden with fruits and vegetables. "You're wasting your time trying to grow tomatoes. Nothing else is growing very good either." Cody sat in a lawn chair, having a beer and had a hose watering the tomatoes she had planted in the dirt she had hauled in next to the cement foundation of their house. The heat from the cement and the consistent watering produced a real good crop that Amber gave Cody credit for.

Cody's interest in gardening had taken off. He hired truckloads of top soil. They cleaned out a horse barn for the manure. Shovel full, by shovel full, they filled up five-gallon buckets and carried them up the incline to dump them into the back of Cody's truck. After hauling the manure home, they shoveled it out in a pile and covered it in black plastic to compost before spreading it on the garden. Very, very labor intensive, but that's what it took to get good crops. Cody, in spite of extremely limited carpentry skills, built a rustic greenhouse. With the improvements, they soon had a good vegetable garden, fruit trees, and the greenhouse full of tomatoes and cucumbers. Amber fully agreed that his involvement made the difference in a much greater harvest. Now, when she planted and weeded, they would keep the garden watered until it was time to harvest. They produced enough of some fruits and vegetables to last through the winter.

Home canning was the cat's meow to take to the mushroom patches along with fresh fruit and vegetables from the garden and greenhouse. Part of the stress to sustain themselves was lifted. Cody fully retired, taking an early pension. Amber kept working for a couple years after she was able to receive her full pension.

They no longer had loan payments, owned their home and vehicles outright, and had time to travel. Keeping active with gardening, fishing, camping, picking wild mushrooms and berries, and going hunting when they gathered their winter firewood supply kept them healthy and in fairly good shape. "Grow old with me, the best is yet to be," wasn't too far from the truth.

# Chapter 31

Cody loved his hockey games and watched his team on television whenever he could.

"Our Montreal Canadians are playing the Las Vegas Knights in Las Vegas. We can get tickets and fly down for a vacation. Henry and Shelly are going. You girls can stay in the casino while Henry and I watch the game live," Cody made the plans for Amber to arrange.

Montreal lost, but the guys were grinning from ear to ear. Cody had worn an authentic old-time Montreal hockey sweater. A young hockey fan asked him if he used to play hockey.

"Sure." Cody decided to go for it. He knew about a lot of hockey players.

"What's your name?" the eager fan asked.

"Larry Robinson, they used to call me Big Bird." Cody grinned... and Henry kept going before he cracked up laughing.

The fan excitedly waved his friends over as he took a quick picture of himself with "Big Bird." Cody quickly high-fived all his fan club and caught up to Henry. The fans figured they met a real live hockey hero. Cody and Henry had an amusing story to tell their friends and family.

When Angela heard the story, she found some pictures of Larry Robinson on the internet to show her parents. Amber was amazed at the resemblance they held to each other from their youth, right to the present time. They both sported a reddish mustache in younger days, white hair as they grew older, and were much the same height and build.

"Dad's famous." Angela laughed. "Maybe he still has a chance with Dolly Parton. It's funny, Carey got mistaken for Wayne Gretzky before too. All Cybil and I get asked is if we're the Queen of Sheba."

Angela and Harold, Carey and Cindy, and Cybil and Everet, with all their (grand) children, planned a Bentley family trip to Hawaii. What a wonderful way to have a family reunion. The condos were overlooking the beach, and they could be in the ocean every day or in the swimming pool. They saw giant turtles right up on the beach. They experienced the road to Hanna, went to a luau, enjoyed the scenery, went fishing, scuba diving, zip-lining, among other activities. They indulged in dinner at Bubba Gump. Hugely expensive, but a priceless time together for family fun and love.

Southern destinations had much warmer winters than Tesley. A week or more there helped the long winters to pass. Cody and Amber discovered all-inclusive trips to Cuba and Mexico that they could afford. They rented a house in Nevada for a month with Henry and Shelly. "Snowbirding" was their new winter hobby. The years kept going by quicker and quicker.

Doctor visits, medications, and body repair and maintenance was becoming commonplace. "Look at those old people," Cody said as an elderly couple walked hand in hand down the steps away from the doctor's office. Seeing Amber's grin, he added with a sigh, "Guess we are too."

Amber urged Cody to stay active in the winter, sure that they would stay younger longer by doing so. Cody did a fair amount of ice fishing with Carey and his friends. Sometimes Amber would go with. Carey devised a metal bucket with air vent holes chopped into the side to carry with enough wood for a warmup campfire that wouldn't leave a mess on the ice. Some days, Cody didn't mind going for a walk to the bridge over the river to look at the fish below it on a sunny day. If it was too cold, Amber often left him to his couch and television to go for a walk in the fresh air by herself. They swore the closets were shrinking their clothes, larger and larger sizes had to be bought.

They'd had fifty years together, spending their anniversary in the pine mushroom camp where good friends surprised them with a beautifully decorated cake and party. They were still facing the future content, hoping for years more of experiences together. They had adjusted to each other. Life was good. Love and laughter the best medicine. If their health held out, maybe they could have ten to thirty more years to celebrate in the same way.

Cody no longer wanted to go anywhere without Amber and expected her to spend the majority of her time with him. Sometimes he depended on her to do things she felt he could do for himself. Other times he would make them both breakfast. They did try to manipulate each other. If she didn't get what he wanted when he wanted it, he claimed he was going to die soon and accused her of not even caring. It didn't help to point out that other people with the same health problems were still active energetic seniors.

Amber wanted to do as much as they could while they still could. They had talked about going to the east coast of Canada, but she no longer counted on it. Warm winter vacations, however, were still very much looked forward to by both. Cody claimed to no longer enjoy picking mushrooms but only going out of love for his wife to make her happy. Once he made it to the mushroom patches, he always caught some of his old enthusiasm. Maybe they couldn't recapture their youth, but they recaptured many good time memories. "Used to be" was one of their often used phrases. Though many people seemed to quit living shortly after they retired, Amber intended for her and Cody to make it close to one hundred years old, staying active and involved with living.

She encouraged their middle-age children to enjoy their youth, reassuring them that they had a long way to go before they would be old. "Dad and I won't even be old for twenty years or more! The warranty may have expired, we might need more maintenance than we used to, but we have a lot of miles left anyhow."

The grandchildren they used to enjoy babysitting were growing into responsible young adults, starting their own careers and families. They had memories of taking them fishing or going for rides on the quad. They'd tried to get them interested in pulling weeds in their garden. They'd built snowmen and went sledding together. They'd gone camping, boating, and swimming. How extremely blessed they were for their health and the health and happiness of all their descendants. They still had time to make more memories with all of them, hopefully. Each generation, though, needs freedom to make their own memories, also.

# Chapter 32

Cody was feeling no pain. "Did you ever see me play the Scottish bagpipes, my dear wife?"

"You don't have bagpipes, Cody!" Amber advised him as she grinned at his playfulness.

Cody grabbed his nose with one hand, put his other hand completely straight, and began hitting himself in the throat as he made a bagpipe tune. It sounded unbelievably like a real bagpipe. So real, that when Amber was able to contain her laughter and wipe the tears from her eyes, she had to try it herself.

Grinning and chuckling, Cody coached her until she could do a passable imitation.

Amber had already eaten the evening meal she had prepared before Cody was ready to eat. She was used to reheating meals for him after he had enough to drink or was finished watching hockey or whatever on TV he wanted to see first. Now it was time to give the bagpipes a rest as Cody declared he was ready for her to dish up his dinner for him. Time for service with a smile.

Cody finished the dinner Amber had reheated for him and roughly grabbed at her. "Now we can go to bed and have sex." He grinned slyly.

"I don't think so," Amber said blandly without anger. "You've had too much to drink for it to work." She would always long to be treated with more respect. He thought his rough rudeness to her was funny even if she suggested he give her a nice hug instead.

"You're probably right," Cody admitted. "I'd have to take a Viagra first." Satisfied that she hadn't actually resisted, rejected, or disrespected him, he promptly fell asleep in his chair by their kitchen table. Soon he was doing the bobble head and breathing through his open mouth. Though it looked completely uncomfortable, it was getting to be a normal evening habit. Later he would wake up enough to lay on the couch to watch TV or stumble carefully to bed. Amber had, for the most part, quit trying to help him make the trip. After a nap, he made it fine by himself and she could avoid his still uncontrolled temper and being groped or swore at. Much as she had once angrily resisted what she thought was disrespectful, she was now resigned to the fact that it would only encourage him to laugh and torment her more if she overly reacted. He did actually love and respect her now, she reasoned. He just had a crude sense of humor at times. Mostly his sense of humor and quick wit still endeared himself to her and the others around him.

Amber had had to toughen up or die. She developed a thicker skin and no longer took things so personally. She learned that venting, without being in the attack mode, helped root out bitterness. They had shared struggles and victories together. They had fought too hard to stay together to ever give up. So many good times and memories were shared and they were still making more. They had married the person of their dreams and gotten through the nightmares.

*Yes,* thought Amber, *there are things I will always hate that we've gone through. There are things we dislike about each other. Maybe things could have been a lot better or a lot worse. The way it is, is the way it is for better or worse. There are things one cannot accept but cannot change either. Maybe wisdom is loving your way through. If only we could live what we believe and truly love our rednecks from start to finish.*

Amber read 1 Corinthians 13:4–8, 13a, "Love is patient, love is kind, and is not jealous, love does not brag, and is not arrogant, does not act unbecomingly; it does not seek its own, is not provoked, does not take into account a wrong suffered, does not rejoice in unrighteousness, but rejoices with the truth; bears all things, endures all things, love never fails…but now abides faith, hope, love, but the greatest of these is love."

In her mind, she added, "A really good sense of humor is a must. We've got a long way to go and a short time to get there, but we're working toward it with God's help. "Happily ever after" stuff takes a lot of ingredients. Tomorrow will be a new adventure to enjoy together. Getting old is not for the faint of heart, but it's still an adventure."

She went to sit by Cody on the couch and watch television with him. He put his arm around her and gave her a hug. "I love you, sweetheart," he said.

"I love you too," Amber replied, "so can we go to the Yukon next spring to pick morels and see more of Canada?" She cuddled against him.

# Behind Closed Doors

I have become acquainted with victims and perpetrators of incest and found it extremely difficult to imagine how it would be possible for otherwise seeming normal and moral persons to carry on with their lives by putting the past behind them. Uncles with their nieces, fathers with their daughters. I know a couple of wives who actually stayed with the guilty husband. The following story is the only imagination I could come up with. Still, "How could they ever forgive themselves?" continues to make me wonder. I cannot imagine the destroyed lives that so many suffered when abuse continued for years.

Sarah woke up on her back in the dark. She had a terrible hangover, nausea welled up inside her. She struggled to roll over so she wouldn't be vomiting all over herself. Lifting her head was next to impossible. As she up-chucked, she pushed herself back from the wretched mess she was making. Finally, there was nothing left in her stomach to empty, though she was still gripped by the involuntary urge and spasms that caused her to gag.

Gradually she became aware that she was on moss in the woods. She was nearly naked, but the rest of her clothes were lying where she had slept. With extreme effort, she reached for them and began to get herself dressed. Exhausted, she lay back down, whimpering, in a fetal position. What had happened? Where was she? How had she gotten into such a state?

She had been at a dance, she remembered. Her girlfriends had wanted her to leave with them, but she was having too much fun dancing and drinking. "I've got my horse, you party poopers! I can take care of myself. Just go!" she insisted. There were at least a couple guys she'd like to get to know better. They seemed to enjoy her personality and wit. Sarah knew she was just a plain and unsought-after girl. She wasn't usually popular at dances but was thrilled to have had steady dance partners last night. That's where her memory quit.

*Oh God! What have I done?* she wondered. *Where am I?* Noise of traffic occasionally passing nearby meant there was a road close by. She unwound from her fetal position and managed to sit up to look around. She grabbed some moss to clean the vomit from her hair and resisted the urge to vomit again and to faint. By sheer will power, she pulled herself upright to lean up against a tree. She could see the road. She was too dizzy to move and rested for several minutes, trying to think.

"Should I try to hitchhike?" She whistled for her horse. "Wait! There's my purse. Please, please let everything still be in it." She carefully lowered herself down from her supporting tree and slowly crawled to her purse. Her money and everything was there! A surge of adrenaline strengthened her as she whistled and stumbled against trees toward the road.

As she got to the road, she recognized her location and allowed herself to rest again out of sight. "Scamper," she called and whistled for her horse, though she was sure it would have headed home on its own by now. She thought she heard a whinny. "Scamper, where are you, boy?" She whistled as loud as she could.

This time Scamper came trotting right to her as he whinnied and nudged her gently. "Oh, Scamper, you saved my life," declared Sarah. Relief flooded through her as she shakily mounted her faithful steed. "Take me home, old boy, and I'll try to stay on you." She closed her eyes and collapsed against his mane with the reins loosely in her hands.

When she again opened her eyes, Sarah realized she must have slept (or passed out), for Scamper was grazing in their yard on the ranch, with her on his back. "It's still dark, so maybe I can sneak us to our beds before my foster parents get worried or angry," she whispered. She and Scamper both had a drink from the brook and Sarah had a quick partial wash and swallowed an aspirin from her purse. She put Scamper in his stall and quietly made it to her own bed.

The next morning, after she showered and dressed in her work clothes, Sarah went quietly into the kitchen. Thankfully, Marie and Peter had left a note that they'd gone to town for supplies and hoped that Sarah would not be lazy about getting her ranch chores done before they got back. Gratefully, she wouldn't have to face them but could have a chance to see if a glass of milk and a piece of toast would settle her stomach. She found an aspirin and forced herself to start on her day by taking care of Scamper's brushing down.

Sarah's shame for her lack of memory bothered her enough that she resisted invites to future parties and drinking. She diligently accomplished the chores Marie and Peter always assigned her. The way Peter stared at her disturbed her. His hugs and caressing touches didn't seem quite fatherly, occurring mainly when Marie was not present. She became determined to do any part-time job that would allow her to save up money so that she could move out on her own as soon as possible. She knew the welfare system paid her foster parents for her care but became increasingly aware that others would pay for the type of work they expected from her.

Over a month had gone by when she realized she hadn't had her period since before the dance where she'd gotten so drunk. She started wearing clothes that hid her shape. Marie was teasing her that they were feeding her too good, because she was gaining weight. Sarah continued to hide the real reason.

Peter followed Sarah through the horse barn as she went about her chores. "I like a woman with a little meat on her bones," he said suggestively. "You've just turned sixteen, but you look ripe, ready to pick." He stroked her face and then put his hands on her shoulders. Just then, Marie came through the barn door. Peter gave Sarah a playful-looking shake and greeted his wife with a smile. "Just telling our girl she's almost grown up now. We're going to miss her in a couple more years if she moves out. Course she could stay and work for her room and board, right?"

Marie agreed, but Sarah had other secret plans she kept silent about. She would tell her case worker about her pregnancy when she could no longer hide it. She would keep the baby if she could and go somewhere else. She really wanted to finish high school.

Maybe Alice, the neighbor who had hired her for spring cleaning help, could give her information about home schooling since she home schooled her twelve-year-old child, Amy, when she worked at a logging camp as the cook, except for spring breakup. Alice's son had left home to be on his own shortly after his father (Alice's husband) had died suddenly of a heart attack. Alice seemed to care and mother her more than her foster parents did and had paid her well whenever she had hired Sarah.

Sarah finished the spring cleaning Alice hired her to do and gratefully accepted the cup of tea that Alice offered her. "Tell me how you are doing, Sarah. What are your plans in a couple more years when you finish high school and are able to decide for yourself what you want to do?" Alice opened the conversation with caring concern.

Suddenly, Sarah found herself tearfully telling Alice how much she wanted to get away from Peter and Marie. How she had gotten drunk at a dance and gotten pregnant without knowing who the father was. She wanted to keep her child and wanted to earn her own way and be on her own, but how on earth could she. She wanted to be able to finish high school by correspondence if she could. She knew she had to talk to her case worker soon, but what could she hope for?

"Oh my!" Alice responded. "I always thought your foster parents used you as a hired hand, but you seemed so hardworking and responsible for someone in the 'system' who never had a chance to experience their own loving family life. Everyone makes mistakes, once in a while, my dear. Let's think on this awhile. Here's a Kleenex. Have another cup of tea before you leave."

Sarah felt like a weight was lifted off her by the time she left to go. Alice would call her again as soon as she could think of a plan to present to Sarah's case worker. Maybe she could figure something out and there was still some hope for her future.

Alice made some phone calls to the office that had hired her as camp cook. She was expected to go back to work after the bush dried out enough for the loggers to start up logging again. The assistant cook (or bull cook) had wanted summer time off, so would they consider a newly pregnant teenager, who was a good willing worker that would be in Alice's charge, to do the job? Since it would only be for two months, they wouldn't be taking as much of a chance as Alice would, if Sarah wasn't as much help as the other bull cook had given her.

"Yes," they decided. It could be the perfect solution for a two-month replacement. They were confident in the reputation Alice had earned as a skilled cook as well as being fair and honest. Alice should let them know as soon as possible if Sarah was going to be available.

Alice accompanied Sarah to consultation with her case worker. Many questions were asked and answered before it was finally agreed that Alice could foster parent Sarah for the future years in foster care. Part of the deciding factors were Sarah's uneasiness with Peter's touches and the obvious affection that Alice and Sarah had for each other. Amy's school records were a credit to the home schooling solution that was presented also.

So it came about that Sarah did very well with her summer job, proving to her employers that she was a willing capable worker. When summer ended and Gary the bull cook came back, Sarah was ready to tackle her schoolwork. She turned seventeen amid jokes from the camp's crew that it didn't look like she'd "never been kissed at sweet sixteen." With Sarah's help, Alice arranged extra baked goods and main dishes to be frozen so that Gary would run the kitchen if Sarah's labor started unexpectedly.

Little Candance Alice was born without complications, and Sarah quickly recovered from the trauma of giving birth. She went back to camp with Alice and Amy and resumed her studies with the extra responsibility of her baby. Candy (Candance) quickly grew strong and healthy and soon expected to be treated as royalty among her attentive subjects. She was the tiny queen of the camp.

By the time Candy said her first word, "Ahhmey," Sarah had finished her high school studies and was soon ready to move out of the foster care system. Gary moved on to greener pastures, so Sarah was promoted to Alice's full-time assistant. Living at camp enabled Sarah to save most of her paychecks.

When queen Candy became old enough to start school, Sarah made the tearful decision to leave her beloved Alice and Amy. Logger

Mark liked how Sarah was a capable hardworking girl and had asked her to marry him. Sarah was so grateful that a man wanted her and her child that she accepted immediately. So Candy and Sarah would move into his home after their quiet justice of the peace marriage.

Sarah seemed to worship the ground that Mark walked on and she couldn't do enough to make him content. Candy simply demanded attention from them both. When the new baby Kenny was born, Candy's nose was out of joint. Her mother seemed to forget that she was the most important one in the family. Candy acted as if Sarah had betrayed her rule of the kingdom and defiantly turned away from Sarah to Mark for comfort.

"You'll always be my princess," Mark reassured her as he protected his son from her jealousy. Candy cuddled into Mark and snuggled against him as she glared at Sarah attending to her unwanted brother.

When Emerald was born to Mark and Sarah, Candy was in high school. She was a popular girl among the boys, knowing how to charm them by building up their egos with her outrageous flirting. She had trouble relating to girls and showed her resentment to any female that challenged her popularity.

Emerald was seen, by Candy, as a challenge to her position as the family princess. She became almost desperate for Mark's attention and was secretly hateful toward Sarah and her siblings when he wasn't looking. When Sarah expressed her concern to Mark, he couldn't believe that the girl he knew as sweetness itself could be capable of any meanness.

Candy brought Mark a strong drink after Sarah and her siblings had gone to bed early. "Relax for a while. You deserve a break, and how about I give you a back rub while you enjoy your break? Mom is always too busy now with Emerald and Kenny to give you the attention you deserve."

The back rub and drink did relax Mark. So when Candy came back from the kitchen with another drink, he grinned at her and sipped it while she resumed her massage. When he finished the drink, she sat on his lap with her arms around his neck and kissed his cheek. "Am I still your princess? Do you still love me?" she asked wistfully.

"You're still the princess that I love." Mark reacted with a big hug and kissed her back on her cheek. Candy kissed Mark on his mouth with seeming invitation. Then suddenly Mark couldn't get enough of her warmth. He kissed her passionately. Candy didn't resist but seemed to kiss him back. It was too late for him to stop, but Candy was not frightened. This was different than the boys she'd played with. "My princess, my princess, my beautiful sweet princess," Mark was mumbling. Afterward, he admonished her not to tell anyone. It would be their precious secret. "Your mother wouldn't understand."

But Candy didn't understand. Mark stayed with her mother and siblings and avoided repeating their intimacy. When Alice and Amy came for a visit, she decided to tell them her version of what had happened. Her revenge would be to break up the family.

Mark tried to explain to Sarah how it had happened, but she couldn't bear it. "Candy is a child even if she tempted you. You are supposed to be her father figure and a responsible adult. How could you destroy our whole family?"

Candy got counselling and Mark got jail time. Sarah took care of her family and supported them as best as she could. Sarah and Candy were constantly arguing. Kenny and Emerald missed their father and didn't understand what had happened. After counselling began taking effect, Candy was able to admit that she had been spoiled by the early unlimited attention in her youth and had just wanted so bad to have it back that she had tried too much to be the most important person in their family.

"I'm sorry for not realizing what I was doing!" Candy stated. "I am going to go out on my own and try to start a new life, I do feel love for you all, but we can't be together anymore. It really wasn't all Mark's fault."

Sarah insisted she didn't need to go, cried, and professed her love and her own guilt in not realizing Candy's needs. The siblings all hugged each other and said they were still family. Still, Candy was sure she must begin healing on her own and so should her family. Step by step, Candy succeeded toward her goals with new love and understanding.

Somehow, no matter what, dirty laundry is always aired around the people who are hurt by it. "Their father is a child molester," was whispered as the children finished their schooling. "Her husband is in jail for molesting his stepdaughter," former friends discarded Sarah. Finally, good memories overcame the life-changing circumstances.

Sarah forgave Mark for what she considered as his affair and wanted him back for her and the children's sake. She felt like she would never be able to attract or find another husband for herself and father for her children. When Mark was released from his jail term, they decided to sell and move to get away from the stories of their past. Mark, being a skilled and dependable logger, found work again. Kenny soon hired on with the same company. Emerald found a man who wanted her for his own precious jewel.

Sarah found her empty nest to be quite lonely. It seemed the past always came back to haunt her no matter where they lived. When Kenny fathered a daughter and married the mother, Sarah loved to babysit. Once again, ugly rumors and whispers of the grandfather being a child molester emerged. Kenny and Emerald had no such fears for their children but trusted Mark and Sarah with them. Still, the rumors were hard to take, and they moved again.

Sarah took a job as assistant camp cook in the camp that Mark worked out of. They sold their home and bought a nice travel trailer, giving their home address as Highway 97 North. Finally, the rumors seemed to have left them alone. But then a new man was hired and came to stay in camp. He had heard of Mark's jail term, and soon the whole camp was buzzing with the rumors. Not only did they label Mark as a child molester but disdained Sarah as an unbelievably unfit mother to stay with the man who had molested her own daughter. It became too uncomfortable for them both. They both quit their jobs and pulled their trailer out of the camp. Highway 97 was calling them again.

They stumbled into a "brain" (false morel) mushroom picking camp as they looked for a place to park their trailer overnight. Friendly pickers and buyers welcomed them. The brains were found in the disturbed ground of past logging blocks. Mark and Sarah soon started making a good wage by joining in the mushroom picking. All the brain mushrooms had to be dried in order not to be toxic. The buyers had large dryer systems set up for the mushrooms they bought. The dried mushrooms would be boxed and shipped to mainly European markets. When the mushrooms began petering out, most of the pickers were pulling out to look for the fire morels. Mark and Sarah were hired to help with the last of the drying and packing up of the acquired brains.

"We're moving our buying station to the big fire in Watson Lake in the Yukon," they urged. "We could really use a couple trustworthy good workers to help with the drying and maybe even be set up as another buyer."

Sarah and Mark liked the idea, especially since the buyers didn't question their background before deciding they were well qualified. They followed the buyers to their new camp.

When the volume of mushrooms warranted another station to be set up in a second location, it was given to Sarah and Mark. Mark was given several thousand dollars, baskets, scale, and buying table and tent to start up. Sarah did the majority of the work, but it was a profitable partnership. Pickers came with baskets of freshly picked morels that Sarah would sort for quality. Then she weighed the mushrooms and paid the pickers, while Mark tied lids on the baskets and stacked the ones for shipping fresh and brought the ones for drying to the drying shack.

Their employers came by to pick up the fresh mushrooms to be sent out by air freight. They brought a drying trailer outfitted with a heater and fan that Sarah and Mark would fill with morels that were spread out on wire racks so the circulating hot air would dry and preserve them. As long as their backgrounds remained a secret, they did a good job and made new friends.

"You can camp next to us so you won't have to worry about anything being stolen while you are out picking." Sarah made friends with a new pair of pickers. Charlie and Louise set up their camp. Mark took time out to instruct them and help them find and identify areas to pick.

Sarah and Mark began to encourage Charlie and Louise to continue their mushroom picking adventures by camping near them for the brain (false morel), fire morels, and the matsutake pine picking seasons.

When the rumors reached Charlie and Louise of Sarah and Mark's past, they found it hard to believe. They didn't drop their friendship entirely but tried to credit them with putting the past behind them and thinking of them as the people they now were. They distanced themselves from becoming closer friends, however, and claimed to set up their future camps in a different area to avoid the busyness of the buying station.

The years of stress took their toll on Sarah's health. She was still used to doing everything she could for Mark, but her body was in constant pain. She swallowed pain killers every day in order to function but cheerfully preformed her tasks without any self-pity.

Then the medical tests done on Sarah came back. She had terminal cancer. Right to the very end, she was more concerned for Mark than for herself. She finished her days with the same courage she had shown throughout her life.

"I'm ready to meet my maker," Sarah reassured Mark and her children as they visited her in her hospital room. "I want you to face your futures with hope and happiness. I love you all, and the best thing you can do for me is to continue on without me and remember our good memories." Sarah seemed still strong and alert.

Her family left for the night, assuring Sarah that they would be back in the morning. Sarah slipped quietly away while they were gone as though she thought it would be easier for them that way.

A new door opened for Sarah as the old door closed behind her at last.

# About the Author

Starting at a young age, observations and imaginations have played a part in the author's desire to read and write books. A busy life has kept her from writing very much until now; in retirement, she finds the time to entertain this dream.

CPSIA information can be obtained
at www.ICGtesting.com
Printed in the USA
BVHW042057291021
620227BV00001B/120